A SPORTING MURDER

Greg McKenzie Mystery No. 5

Chester D. Campbell

First Edition

10 9 8 7 6 5 4 3 2 1

Cover design by Michael Hicks and Beth Terrell

Printed in the United States of America

Library of Congress Control Number: 2010907655

ISBN 978-0-9846044-0-1

Night Shadows Press, LLC
8987 E. Tanque Verde #309-135
Tucson, AZ 85749-9399

Also by Chester D. Campbell

Greg McKenzie Mysteries:

The Marathon Murders
Deadly Illusions
Designed to Kill
Secret of the Scroll

Sid Chance Mysteries:

The Surest Poison

For my long-time Scottish friend, Betty McClellan, faithful supporter from the start, who provided the inspiration for some of Greg's background.

Author's Notes and Acknowledgments

First a bit of explanation about the adventures of Greg and Jill McKenzie, and this book in particular. The first book took place in November of 2002, the second a year later, the third the following spring, the fourth that summer, and now this one around Christmas. So in Greg-time, it's still 2004. To avoid confusion, I call the location where the Nashville Predators play simply "the arena." In 2004 it was the Gaylord Entertainment Center. Now it's the Bridgestone Arena. Also, the Homicide Division back then worked out of the Criminal Justice Center. Now homicide detectives have been spread out among the precincts, much to many people's chagrin .

I have several to thank for their help with this book. The character Louie Aregis is named after the 6th degree black belt owner of Aregis Taekwondo in Goodlettsville (Nashville suburb), where grandson Justin Jones qualified for his probationary black belt while this was being written. Aregis wanted to be a bad guy. Michael Bunch of the Nashville Fire Department, a certified arson investigator, provided help with the bombing scenario. Rudy Kalis, sports director of WSMV Channel 4 in Nashville, gave advice on the local sports scene. A source who prefers to remain anonymous gave me some valuable insights into the background of the local criminal element. Forensic guru Dr. Doug Lyle helped with a poison question.

Invaluable assistance in critiquing parts of the manuscript was provided by my colleagues in the Quill & Dagger Writers Guild: Beth Terrell, Cathy Randall, Nancy Sartor, Nicole Nelson-Hicks, Nina Fortmeyer, and Richard Emerson. A special kudo to the team of Michael Hicks and Beth Terrell for the striking cover.

For putting up with my sometimes unfathomable antics during the creation of this book, while attempting to maintain some sort of order among the surroundings, I must express my highest regard for my wife, Sarah. Thanks for everything.

 **1**

WHEN YOU GET a strange feeling that something isn't quite right, even though there's no obvious basis for it, your comfort index begins a slow slide, like a worn tire on an icy road. You have no idea where it might end up but know it won't be someplace you want to go. That's how I felt after getting the call from Arnold Wechsel on Saturday afternoon the week before Christmas.

Jill and I had spent a few hours at the office that morning, tidying up loose ends to clear the deck for the new case we had taken on the day before. A brisk north wind that bore the sharp sting of winter chased us back to our warm and cozy log cabin in the woods. I don't mean to sound like some latter-day Abe Lincoln; it was closer to a manor than a country cottage. As for the woods, think a forested three-acre plot in a heavily-populated Nashville suburb.

I had just pulled off the padded jacket that made me resemble an Iditarod driver who'd wandered off course when the phone rang. I checked the caller ID and saw Arnold's name. We hadn't heard from the young man in a couple of months.

"Where've you been, Arnold?" I asked. "Long time no see."

"I have been working many hours," he said, his German accent making it sound like "verking."

"Your Uncle Jeff has been pretty quiet lately, too," I said. Arnold's Aunt Lisle was married to Jeff Price, an old Air Force OSI colleague now stationed at Ramstein Air Base in Germany.

"I talk to my *mutter* every week or two."

His mother was Lisle Price's younger sister. Three years ago they had paid his way to study the maintenance of high performance vehicles at Nashville Auto Diesel College.

"I hope everyone is doing well over there," I said.

"Yes, thank you." A man of few words, he got right to the point. "I am calling for a special reason, Mr. McKenzie. I have some important information for you."

From my limited experience with him, I knew Arnold was a serious young man. Now he sounded downright mysterious. "What sort of information?"

"I do not wish to talk about it on the telephone."

"Then come on over. We just got home and don't plan to go anywhere else." We had invited him for dinner once, so he knew where we lived.

"Not there. I do not want it known that we meet."

This was beginning to get spooky. "What does it concern?"

He hesitated, then said, "Your National Basketball Association matter."

I couldn't believe what I'd just heard. My voice sharpened. "Arnold, how did you know we had any interest in that situation?"

"Please, I will tell everything when we meet. It will, how do you say, blow the mind."

I looked around at Jill and shook my head. "When and where?"

"Seven-thirty tonight. I will be at a small automobile repair shop owned by my friend. It will be closed, but he gives me the key."

Arnold provided me an address in the Dickerson Pike area of Northeast Nashville and promptly hung up.

Jill saw my puzzled look. "What was that all about?"

I told her what Arnold had said.

"How do you suppose he knew about our case?" she asked. "We haven't even met the principals yet."

"That's something I intend to ask him when we meet. It sure sounds like the situation Terry mentioned, though."

Terry Tremont, McKenzie Investigations' best lawyer client, had called us in yesterday afternoon. He was retained by a group of Nashville Predators' hockey fans circling the ice wagons in an effort to thwart a clique of local businessmen intent on bringing an NBA team to Music City. It was the old story of this town ain't big enough for the both of us. Or, in this case, the three of use, since Nashville already had both professional football and ice hockey.

Terry wanted us to check into a rumor that something shady was going on among the NBA franchise seekers. He had been frank in laying out his skepticism. He thought his clients' concerns were based on flimsy evidence.

"Somebody heard bits of a conversation and told somebody else," Terry had said. "Could be strictly a rumor, but these people are fanatics. They're really fired up about this, so we need to try and find some answers."

From Arnold's description of information that would blow my mind, it certainly sounded like he was ready to confirm the rumor.

"He didn't give me much chance to ask questions," I said.

Jill moved into the kitchen and filled the carafe with water to make coffee. "You probably wouldn't have gotten any answers, dear. Arnold is a sweet boy, but he can be awfully reticent."

"I'm getting some bad vibes from this," I said.

Jill spooned coffee into the filter and flipped the switch. "If this has the potential to solve our case, you should be getting good vibes."

I sat at the kitchen table and gazed about at the miniature

Christmas tree on the long white tile counter, plus numerous other holiday doo-dads my bride of nearly forty years had artfully placed around the room. It was the season for good vibes. I just didn't have them.

"I wish we'd been able to talk with one of Terry's clients before now," I said. "What did you get set up with Bradley Smotherman?"

"His secretary said we could see him at eight-thirty on Monday. He's in one of those office buildings on West End out past Centennial Park."

Smotherman was ringleader of the group called Protect our Preds, the super hockey fans we would be working with.

"Did you have any luck with Gordon Franklin or Mack Nolan?" I asked.

She ran slender fingers through her thick black hair, a feature that, along with a pleasantly-curvy body, sometimes made people mistake her for my daughter. Not an ego-soothing notion. She was nearly as old as I was. "Franklin will see us Monday at eleven-thirty. Mack Nolan, as you might guess, will be harder to pin down. I talked to his manager. He promised to make time for us as soon as possible."

I understood. With a string of top country hits, the young man was much in demand around the circuit. He, along with the other two well-heeled fans, had put up most of the money for the organization. They had hired Terry Tremont and planned various strategies in an attempt to thwart the basketball promoters. Being primarily a Tennessee Titans fan, I wasn't prepared to take sides on the issue. But if Arnold held the key to clearing up the claims of skullduggery, I anxiously awaited hearing him out.

 **2**

I DISLIKED THE PLACE as soon as I stepped out of the car, my breath vaporizing in the cold December night as though I had lapsed back into the smoking habit. Rather than smoke, the smell of used oil and worn tires tainted the breeze. The street appeared as cluttered as the back room in a neighborhood bar. Iron rods criss-crossed the window of the small auto repair shop that had been a service station in a previous life. In a half-hearted attempt at Christmas décor, a winking string of icicle lights writhed like a nervous snake above the overhead door.

A shiny red Corvette several years removed from the showroom sat next to the building. Arnold Wechsel had driven it when he visited our house. I saw no lights inside but knew he had to be here. I was running a few minutes late. As I approached the office door, hands jammed into the warmth of my jacket pockets, I regretted not bringing my 9mm Sig Sauer. Like most PI's, I didn't carry it routinely. I had been a bit lax in my thinking tonight, though, feeling Arnold's imposing size would keep any bad guys at bay.

At the door I hesitated, then turned the knob.

I pulled the door open, stared into the darkness. Something began to take shape on the floor as my eyes adjusted. I drew back, half expecting a bark or a lunge. Instead, I realized it was a body. I felt a pounding in my chest. Was it Arnold?

My first impulse was to rush in and turn on a light. My cop instinct restrained me. Not without a weapon.

I hurried out to my Grand Cherokee for a flashlight. Back at the door, I shined the light inside. Worn black and white vinyl tiles covered the floor. One white square was tinged a garish red. Arnold Wechsel lay sprawled on his back beside a battery display, a lifeless stare fixed on the ceiling.

I caught my breath and my heart seemed to stop. I swept the area with the flashlight but saw no one. Moving carefully to his side, I squatted down and checked his pulse. Nothing. A large, stocky young man with a neck like a Titans lineman, Arnold had fallen almost the full depth of the office. A small round hole in his cheek with dark smudging around it told me he had been shot. Blood pooled beneath his head from the exit wound.

I felt totally helpless.

Jeff Price's wife and sister-in-law had been happy that a friend was nearby in Nashville to offer help if needed. In the back of my mind, I knew this was not my fault, but I felt responsible anyway. He had come here to give me information he thought I needed.

My investigator mindset kicked in and I knew what I had to do. Find who killed Arnold Wechsel. I pulled out my cell phone and speed-dialed my Homicide buddy, Detective Phillip Adamson.

"Phil, this is Greg McKenzie," I said.

"Damn, Greg. You really know how to spoil a guy's nap." He spoke slowly, as if grappling with clouds that needed clearing.

"Sorry, friend. This is one call I really wish I didn't have to make."

He suddenly sounded wide awake. "What's happened?"

"I was supposed to meet a young German who's the

nephew of an old OSI colleague. He was bringing me some information. When I got here, I found him shot in the face. Dead."

"Damn. Where are you?"

I gave him the address, explained the condition of the body, the darkened shop office.

"I'll get a patrol car and an ambulance over there."

"Thanks."

"You carrying?"

"No."

"In that area, on a Saturday night?"

"Not my smartest move lately."

"That's for sure. Stay in your car until they get there. I'll be right behind 'em."

I took a last look at Arnold, already dreading the call to Jeff Price at Ramstein. The Metro Police chaplain would contact the family, but I needed to alert Jeff when things settled down. I pulled the door shut, walked over and placed my hand on the hood of the sleek red car, using a handkerchief to avoid disturbing any fingerprints, or leaving any of my own. Still warm, despite the frigid air. I glanced at my watch. Seven-forty-three. He hadn't been here long. Was he a target of opportunity for some young punk out to grab a quick buck? If so, the killer would have high-tailed it out of here. Or had someone been waiting to ambush him? In that case, the murderer could still be around.

I got in my Jeep and pressed the door lock. Would anybody have heard the shot, I wondered? I looked around the darkened street. A drab market that likely depended on the sale of beer and cigarettes for survival sat to one side, closed for the day. A vacant building in the other direction had a For Lease sign in place of its former occupant's name. Across the street, a blue tarp stretched over the roof of a burned-out house. The nearest occupied residence appeared a couple of doors down, where a bare bulb with a few years of grunge on it cast a dim glow over the porch. Not the sort of area where people would come out and volunteer information even if a cannon had been fired.

I took out my cell phone and made another call I dreaded. When Jill answered, I tried to put it gently. "I've got some bad news, babe. When I got here, I found Arnold had been shot."

"Oh, Greg! That's awful. Is it bad?"

There was no way to make it any easier. "As bad as it gets."

"You mean he's..."

"Dead," I said when she hesitated. "Phil Adamson and more cops are on the way."

"His mother will be devastated." After a moment of pained silence, she asked, "Who could have done it?"

"That's what I intend to find out."

"Do you have your gun?"

"No. Coming to meet with Arnold, I didn't see the need for it." Though I should have, considering the location.

"Be careful, dear, and don't do anything rash."

I liked to think of myself as a guy who chooses the prudent alternative, although expedience sometimes seems to get in the way. I didn't make any promises. My wife knows me too well for me to try blowing smoke in her direction.

I heard the sirens before I got off the phone. Shortly afterward, I found myself flanked by two Metro Nashville Police blue and whites. I got out with my PI card in hand. A burly, stern-faced cop with a thick mop of white hair confronted me. From the look on his face, I gathered he was not at all happy that I had forced him out in the cold away from a warm, cozy corner café.

I held out the card. "I'm Private Investigator Greg McKenzie."

He gave my ID a cursory glance. "They told me you'd be here. Where's the body and what happened?" The tone of voice told me this was not a guy to mess with.

I read "Dexter" on his name plate, then pointed toward the shop entrance. "He's just inside that door. He's been shot in the face."

The sound of another siren cut through the cold night air. The cop looked around as a boxy Metro Fire Department ambulance swerved into the parking area and added it's flashing lights to the Christmas tree effect of the police cars.

"Hadn't we better check out the building?" a low-pitched female voice asked from behind me.

I turned to see the blue uniform of the second cop, who had stood silently behind me. She was a little shorter than my five-ten and a lot slimmer. I judged her to be mid-to-late twenties.

"You see anybody else around here, McKenzie?" Officer Dexter asked. It sounded more like a demand.

"No."

"How long you been here?"

"Around fifteen minutes. I didn't see anyone, but they could have gone out the back."

"You didn't go inside?"

"Only to check his pulse. I didn't find any."

"Come on, Bolling," he said. "You stay where you are, McKenzie. I'll get back to you."

The officers drew their guns and headed for the building in a cautionary crouch as two men climbed out of the ambulance, one carrying a large equipment bag.

"What do we have here?" a tall paramedic asked, zipping up his blue jacket against the icy breeze. He had the physique of a basketball center and the weary expression of someone who'd rather be back at the fire station drinking coffee instead of traipsing around in this God-awful cold.

I explained what I had found, that the cops were clearing the building. As the ambulance crew ambled toward the shop, I headed back to my car. I didn't see any advantage to standing out here freezing. As I slid onto the seat, I realized I'd not had a chance to consider the repercussions of this murder on our case. Before I could get my mind shifted away from the shock of finding Arnold dead, the cell phone rang.

"I'm headed out North First," Phil Adamson said. "Are you okay?"

"I've been better."

"Hang in there. I'll be on in a jiffy. Patrol guys on the scene?"

"Guy and gal," I said. "Dexter and Bolling."

"Watch your flanks, buddy. Tom Dexter's a real hardass. He give you any problems."

"Not yet."

"Give him time."

"I wasn't too pleased with the way he delivered his 'I'll get back to you.'"

Phil chuckled. "Try to keep from getting cuffed before I can make it over there."

He was familiar with my reputation for not treading lightly on toes that got in the way. I stuck the phone back on my belt and looked up to see the older cop stalk out of the shop headed for my Jeep. Evidently he'd left the young policewoman to monitor the crime scene. I donned my Tennessee Titans cap and stepped out onto the asphalt.

"Find anybody else?" I asked.

"No. You know the victim?"

"His name is Arnold Wechsel."

"Who is Wechsel and what's he to you?"

Where his face had looked stern before, he twisted it into a scowl now.

"He's the nephew of a former Air Force colleague of mine. He called this afternoon and asked me to meet him here at seven-thirty tonight."

"What for?"

"He said he had some information for me."

"About what?"

"He said he'd tell me when we met."

"You make a habit of this, McKenzie? Traipsing around at night in shitty places with no idea why?"

"Officer Dexter, I worked a quarter of a century as a special agent for the Air Force Office of Special Investigations. I've spent many a night meeting with informants, having no idea what sort of info they might show up with."

"I don't give a damn if you've spent a hundred years meeting with pimps and whores. I want to know what you were doing here tonight. And don't tell me you were just fishing."

I couldn't see the handcuffs on his belt, but I knew they were there. And though I had no desire to try them on, I'd had about enough of his blustering.

I took a deep breath. "I just talked to Detective Phil Adamson on the phone. He was on North First and said he'd be here in a jiffy. Why don't we wait for him and I can satisfy everyone's curiosity with one telling?"

"Are you refusing to answer my question?"

I'm sure he wasn't accustomed to anyone crossing him. I suspected the flush in his face did not just stem from the weather. He seemed to be near the boiling point. And so was I.

"No, sir. I'm not refusing anything," I said in a slow, deliberate voice. "I'm merely suggesting—"

"Bullshit!"

 **3**

DEXTER AND I faced each other like a couple of duelers ready to fire as Phil's white Chevrolet Malibu screeched to a halt nearby. Tall and gaunt with a beak of a nose and a dour look that made him resemble a bird of prey, Phil Adamson was a veteran detective I had befriended, after a rocky start, before I got into the PI business. Since then we had collaborated on several cases, including one where we stared into the barrel of a 9mm semiautomatic held by a remorseless assassin.

Phil hurried over to where Dexter and I stood. "What's the situation, Tom?" he asked.

"We got a dead one on the floor in there," the officer said. He nodded his head toward the building. "Paramedics just checked him."

"I've already alerted the Medical Examiner's office. They have somebody on the way. Is Bolling inside?"

"Right. I left her in charge and came out to talk to this so-called investigator."

"For your information, Officer Dexter," Phil said, his voice calm but unyielding, "Greg McKenzie was responsible for solving the Marathon Motor Works case a few months back. Nailed the guy who killed three people." He turned to me. "I'll talk to you in a few minutes. Let me get in here and get a report from the officers."

Dexter twisted his mouth in obvious anger but followed Phil toward the shop without further comment. I'm sure he knew he was dealing with a real pro in Adamson. Besides twenty years experience as a detective, Phil had a criminal justice degree and taught the subject at a local community college.

I returned to my car and prepared to hibernate as the parking lot began to take on the look of a police convention. Crime scene techs, a patrol sergeant, more blue and whites, the Medical Examiner's man. I spent my time trying to reconcile the grief I felt at Arnold's death with a growing determination to track down his killer. Phil had the responsibility to find who did it, but I had a personal stake in solving the crime.

When Phil came out, he opened the passenger door and slid into my Jeep. "Sorry to keep you waiting. How long have you known Wechsel?"

"Close to a year, I guess. When Jeff Price talked to my old commander and found out I was in Nashville, he called and told me about his new wife's nephew. They'd only been married for a year. Arnold studied high performance cars at Nashville Auto Diesel College."

"You said he was bringing you some information. Was it related to a case you're working?"

"Right. I can't discuss it, though. We're working this one for a lawyer, Terry Tremont of the Three Tees."

Normally, a PI's investigation is subject to police scrutiny, but when it's done on behalf of an attorney, it's privileged.

Phil scratched his nose. "Tremont, Tisley and Tarwater. They seem to like you. Give me a hint, at least."

"It involves that NBA deal."

His normal frown turned darker. "You mean your friend got croaked over a basketball franchise?"

"I don't know what it means, Phil." I threw up my hands. "I wondered if it might be a simple robbery."

"Doesn't appear to be."

"We just got called in yesterday. Haven't even talked to the principals involved."

"How come you met at this Godforsaken place?"

"I certainly wouldn't have picked it. It was Arnold's idea. Seems the owner is a friend who gave him the key."

"I'd better get hold of the owner of this place and see if he can tell me anything else about what's going on."

He turned toward the door.

"Did he have any papers on him?" I asked. "Anything he might have been bringing to me?"

Phil looked over his shoulder. "Nothing but a billfold stuffed with cash. Was this a payoff?"

"Hardly. Look, Phil. I've got a personal stake in this one. Keep me in the loop. Okay?"

"I'll do what I can. You know you're lucky you didn't get here early for that appointment. There might have been two dead guys in there."

I knew, and I thought about that on the way home.

JILL WAS BREWING steaming cups of spiced tea when I got home. I could have used a Scotch and soda but didn't complain as we sat in front of our massive stone fireplace to discuss what had happened. With the flashing Christmas tree lights and all the baubles and garlands that decorated the room, a festive mood would have seemed appropriate. It was anything but.

"I still can't believe this," Jill said. "He was so quiet and well-mannered."

"I agree. He's the last person you'd think would end up like this."

She sipped at her spiced tea, a troubled look on her face. "Do you think it was related to what he planned to tell you about the NBA deal?"

"I can't say for sure, but it looks that way. He didn't want to talk about it on the phone, and he didn't want anyone to know he was meeting with me. Obviously, someone did."

"Are you going to call Jeff?" she asked.

"I'll have to." I checked my watch. "It's not five in the morning yet over there. I don't want to wake a guy up with news like this."

"Did Phil find anything to indicate who might have been the killer?"

"Not that I'm aware of. I'll have to check back with him after he gets all the crime scene reports, and the autopsy. One thing's for sure. What Terry Tremont's clients heard was not just a rumor. If it's enough to blow my mind and get Arnold killed, something is definitely not right."

Our discussion was interrupted by the telephone on the end table beside the sofa. It was Wes Knight, a newspaper reporter I had met shortly after Jill and I started the agency a year ago. He was an old hand in Nashville, while I was a relative newcomer. Meaning he had sources I needed. When Wes started probing, it could be a bit uncomfortable, but he was not someone I wanted to alienate.

"What's going on, Greg?" he asked. "The cops identified you as the guy who found a murder victim out Dickerson Pike."

"Unfortunately, it's true."

"How did it happen?"

"Sorry, but I can't tell you anything else, Wes. The young man called and asked me to meet him out there. Said he had some information for me."

"That's it?"

"When I arrived, all I found was a body lying on the floor."

"What kind of information did he have?"

"As I told the cops, I have no idea. He didn't tell me on the phone. That's all I know."

"Damn, buddy. You can really get into some scrapes. Hasn't been all that long since you got mixed up in that Marathon Motor Works business."

"True. And we really appreciated your help on that one."

"No problem. How about letting me know if you get any more information about this deal. Remember, you said I was 'J for juicy' on your speed dial."

"I'll let you know if I hear anything juicy," I said, forcing a laugh.

When I put down the phone, Jill looked around at me. "I trust you had your fingers crossed."

"Fingers, toes, anything else, babe. I think I'd better check another news source, though. Maybe one of the TV sports guys. We need to know what goes on inside the professional sports franchise business. It's getting deadly."

I WAITED UNTIL MIDNIGHT to call Jeff Price. He had been up only a short time.

"You're staying up late, Colonel," he said in his Alabama drawl. "It's still Saturday night over there, isn't it?"

"Sure is," I said. "I waited to call so I wouldn't wake you up. I'm afraid I have some bad news."

"What's happened?"

In all my years of passing along emotionally distressing information to family members, I never learned a way to sugarcoat it. "It's about Arnold, Jeff. He called and asked me to meet him last night. When I got there, I found him shot through the head."

"Aw, no..."

I told him what had happened and the circumstances leading up it. He understood. Jeff and I went back quite a few years, to my first assignment as a Special Agent in Charge. His first wife had died before he was assigned to Ramstein, which was located near Kaiserslautern, Arnold's hometown. New wife Lisle worked for a local police agency, where Jeff met her.

"This is gonna kill his mother," Jeff said. "How did he learn this information about your pro basketball deal?"

"He wouldn't tell me on the phone, and I never had a chance to talk to him again." In hindsight, I knew I should have insisted.

"He was a sharp kid, really gung ho on auto racing, but I never heard him mention anything about basketball."

I recalled the night Arnold came over for dinner. "He didn't talk a lot, but it was obvious he enjoyed working at the shop where they build and repair race cars."

"Right. He was pretty high on that job. When he was home the last time, he told me, confidentially, didn't want his mom to know, that he'd done a little gambling on the auto races."

"That's interesting. The homicide detective investigating the case said Arnold had a lot of money in his billfold."

"So the motive obviously wasn't robbery."

"Right."

"Greg, would you do me a favor?"

"I know what you mean," I said. "And it's a given. Us old Air Force guys stick together. I intend to find out who murdered your nephew."

When I climbed into bed a short time later, that promise weighed heavily on my mind.

 4

WE LIVED IN HERMITAGE, a bedroom suburb named for President Andrew Jackson's historic mansion. The impressive home attracted thousands of visitors yearly to the nearby estate. Our office occupied a small space in a strip center a few miles away on the circumferential boulevard that bore the general's nickname, Old Hickory. One of the things I loved about Nashville was the seemingly endless historical snippets that turned up when you peeked below the surface.

On a normal Sunday morning, we would have headed to Gethsemane United Methodist Church, but after last night's shocking debut, I was anxious to start digging into this case. I hoped it would lead to some answers about who had killed Arnold Wechsel. When we arrived at the office around eight, the answering machine chirped with a message to call Terry Tremont. I draped my jacket on the back of my chair and slid in behind my Plain Jane wooden desk, a clone of the one Jill occupied nearby, part of our equal opportunity policy.

"What's the deal on this Arnold Wechsel I read about in the morning paper?" Terry asked when I got him on the line. "The story said he was bringing you some information. Did it by chance relate to our case?"

"Definitely," I said. "When he called, he said he had information about the NBA deal that would blow my mind."

"Damn. What was it?"

"Unfortunately, he wouldn't tell me on the phone. I didn't have a chance to talk to him in person."

Terry listened quietly as I explained what had happened. A bear of a man with a vice-like handshake, a genuinely nice guy, Terry worked out of a downtown office set up to resemble a living room. It had a plush white sofa and chairs arranged around a dark wooden coffee table. A faux fireplace sat against one wall. His "desk" was a small walnut table in a corner of the room. The rationale for the setup was that he liked to work in the comfort of home. I guessed that's where he was calling from now.

"So you think Wechsel had information that would confirm this rumor business," Terry said. "According to the paper, Wechsel came from Germany a few years ago to attend the Auto Diesel College. I'd think they had plenty of that sort of school over there."

I told him about my OSI buddy and how Arnold had wound up in Nashville as Jill dropped the morning newspaper on my desk, folded to the Wechsel murder story.

"Phil Adamson is working the homicide," I said. "I'll try to find out as much as I can from him. Hopefully the trail will lead us toward the information we're looking for. What I need to know is if you've told anybody else about us."

Terry paused a moment. "I called Brad Smotherman and asked him to inform the others. As for anybody else, just my secretary."

"Would you check with her?" I asked. "Find out if she might have mentioned it to anyone else. We have appointments with both Smotherman and Gordon Franklin tomorrow. We'll question them about it. We need to find out how Wechsel got wind of us being involved in this NBA situation."

"Somebody must have let it slip."

"Yeah. With disastrous consequences."

His voice held a somber note. "This gives the issue a whole new dimension, doesn't it?"

"We're not positive the murder was related to the case, but it certainly looks that way. If it was, we've got a lot more precarious situation on our hands."

"I'm glad I got you and Jill on board," Terry said. "In addition to this new turn of events, I've got my wife to contend with. She's demanding to know what we were doing to put the damper on these NBA folks. She's almost as big a Predators fanatic as Smotherman and his crowd."

When I got off the phone, I took a closer look at the newspaper story. It covered the homicide and its aftermath fairly well. I found nothing significant that I didn't already know.

Jill looked across at me. "You told Terry you'd try to get all you could out of Phil Adamson. Is that our next move?"

"Since we can't follow up with our Preditors contacts until tomorrow, that looks like the best we can do for the moment."

I got my detective friend on the phone and asked how his new homicide investigation was going.

"Slowly," he said.

"Did you find the auto shop owner?"

"Yeah, but he wasn't much help."

"My guess is he was an old Auto Diesel College classmate."

"You guessed right. Name is Pete Lara. Actually, Pedro Lara. He's Mexican. Not real good on his English. Said he had no idea what Wechsel was talking about when he called you."

I leaned back and propped my foot on a desk drawer. "Did he know where Wechsel got his money?"

"Just the job working on race cars. I plan to talk with him again, maybe bring along a Hispanic officer and see if I can get more out of him."

"Did you find anything helpful at Wechsel's apartment?"

"We're still going over it. Oddly enough, it wasn't the usual trashy mess of a young bachelor. The place was very neat. His bank records were all carefully filed in a box. One interesting thing, they included several fairly large cash deposits in recent months. Nothing to show where they came from, though. He also made a few pretty good size withdrawals. The computer guys are digging into his laptop. Hopefully we'll pick up something useful."

"I can give you something," I said.

"Oh?"

"I talked to my OSI buddy in Germany. He said Arnold had talked to him about gambling on auto racing. I hadn't even thought about placing bets on auto races, but with the popularity of the sport, it's probably big."

"I've heard of it but not sure how it works. That could be where those bank deposits came from. Did your friend know anything about Wechsel's relationship to pro basketball?"

"I asked about that. He said the boy hadn't mentioned anything."

"Let me know if you hear something else I can use," Phil said.

And the same to you, I thought. But I knew I was lucky to get as much as I had. Phil's friendship went only so far when it dealt with closely held details of an active case. It was the old quid pro quo. You tell me and I'll tell you.

"Do you know when they'll release the body to the family?" I asked.

"When the Medical Examiner gets through with all his cutting and probing. Hopefully they're not too busy and can get the autopsy done today."

When I got off the phone, Jill gave me what I took as a hopeful look. "What did you learn of interest to us?"

"I think we need to visit Mr. Pete Lara, owner of the garage where I found Wechsel's body. He's Mexican, so you'd better brush up on your Español."

After I retired from the Air Force, we had wandered around the U.S. for a while, then spent some time in a jacaranda-scented American military retirement community around Guadalajara, Mexico. Jill picked up the language a lot easier than I did.

"What did Lara tell Phil?"

"Not much. But immigrants, even legal ones, tend to talk more freely to people who aren't cops."

 **5**

I HAD A HUNCH Pete Lara might be at his shop today to clean up the mess. When I called, he answered. I told him I was the one who found Arnold's body and I needed to come out and talk to him. He agreed to cooperate if it would help find who killed his friend.

We headed for the Dickerson Pike area and found the small auto repair shop much as it had appeared last night, although with no police cars or ambulances, the décor lacked all the flashing red, white and blue embellishment. Daylight did little to spruce up the neighborhood. The tired buildings looked as drab as ever beneath a leaden sky. A badly bruised car in need of a new paint job sat in front of the garage, awaiting its turn at some sort of rejuvenation. I parked near the door beside a recent model Chevy with a crumpled front fender.

Inside, the first thing I noticed was the floor tiles had been scrubbed to a shiny black and white. The smell of a disinfectant cleaner hung in the air. A short, stocky young man with bronzed skin and slick black hair stood at a small counter. He was making change from a cash register for a slim black youth with a rear-facing ball cap. Evidently Lara had decided to take customers today since he was here. The boy gave me a stare as he started out.

"That your red Chevy out front?" I asked.

"Yeah."

"Looks like you had a little problem with a fender," I said.

He grinned and tugged at his cap. "A mailbox hit me. One of them big brick jobs. You gotta watch them monsters. They're mean."

Jill and I broke out laughing as he sauntered out.

The mechanic approached us with a hesitant smile. He wore blue coveralls with a dark oily spot on one leg. "You have problem I can help with?"

"I'm Greg McKenzie and this is my wife, Jill. I called you about what happened last night."

The atmosphere changed instantly. His eyes widened into large, dark orbs. "Greg McKenzie," he said in a whisper. "Arnold tell me you come. The police ask why. I don't know."

"I don't either," I said, emphasizing it by spreading my hands. I explained the phone call I received the previous afternoon. "Did he give you any hint of what he wanted to talk to me about?"

He shook his head vigorously. "Private talk. He very mysterious sometimes. I let him use place before. We work together...auto diesel school."

"Did he meet people here often?"

He shrugged. "Sometimes."

"When did you last see Arnold?"

"Yesterday. He come get key."

"How did he seem?"

"Seem?" Lara tilted his head with a puzzled look? "*No comprende.*"

I spoke slowly. "Was he in a good mood? Did he look worried?"

"He no look happy."

"Did he say why?"

"No."

"He was a mechanic at a shop that builds and repairs race cars. Do you know if he also worked at some other job?"

"He never say. He have plenty money."

I thought of what Jeff Price had told me. "Did he like to gamble, do some betting?"

Lara shoved his hands in his pockets. "He ask me if I like make bet. I say no. I spend money on what I see, hold in hand."

"Smart man," Jill said.

"Did he take bets from other people?" I asked.

"He no talk about it."

"Did he ever mention any other close friends, people he may have worked with?"

"Nobody at auto shop."

"Maybe someone he'd met somewhere else?"

He shook his head slowly, looking down at his feet. I'm sure it had been a traumatic day for him. When he glanced up, his eyes widened as with a sudden thought. "Man named Dick..." After a pause, he said what sounded like "oo-your-ee."

"Is that spelled U-L-L-E-R-Y?" Jill asked.

"*Sí*. Yes, yes."

I glanced at her and rumpled my brows. "Thanks."

"Arnold say he do something with race cars," Lara said.

When we were back in the Jeep, Jill took out the ruled pad she used for note taking. "I wonder what those other meetings Wechsel had were about?"

"Would be interesting to know."

"Shall we track down Mr. Oo-your-ee?"

"Thank goodness your Spanish is better than mine. Let's do an online search. First we need to take a look at that apartment where Wechsel lived."

WE DROVE OUT TO Antioch after stopping for lunch. This suburb on the south side of town looked like apartment city. It was littered with projects of all sizes, from fancy gated communities to small, cracker-box structures. They appeared to be popular with the young moderate income set. Arnold Wechsel had lived near Percy Priest Lake in a fashionable red brick building with a covered entrance for each cluster of four units, two up, two down. Several tarp-covered Sea-Doo watercraft occupied slots in the parking area. Small but colorful patches of winter-blooming pansies dotted the grounds. We found Arnold's apartment upstairs, still draped with yellow and black crime scene tape. A knock at the door across from his brought the appearance of a young redhead in ragged jeans and a faded brown tee shirt. She was probably around thirty. She looked us up and down with an appraisal that seemed to say you two are out of your element. I wouldn't have argued the point.

I handed her a business card. "We're private investigators looking into the death of your neighbor, Arnold Wechsel."

"What happened to him was awful," she said. She made exaggerated movements of her mouth like someone practicing to be a public speaker. "I don't know what else you'd want from us, though. The cops have already been here and grilled us like hamburger."

"I'm sure we'll be a bit more tender than the police," I said. "We just have a few questions. May we come in?"

She had a naturally attractive face, until she frowned. "My husband doesn't like me to invite people in when he's not here."

"I doubt that he'd object to us," Jill said, holding out her PI credentials. "We're licensed by the state."

The woman looked at it, then glanced up at me. "You got one?"

I showed her my ID.

"Come on in," she said.

We followed her inside. A neat arrangement of furniture upholstered in pale green faced a large-screen TV. From her sloppy appearance, I was a bit surprised at the look of the apartment. We sat on the sofa across from her. I gave my wife a slight nod since she was our designated female interrogator.

"How long have you known Mr. Wechsel?" Jill asked.

"He'd only been here a few months, but I ran into him now and then. He came and went a lot. Seemed like a decent enough sort of guy. He was big. Friend of mine on the bottom floor called him a handsome brute. Said his hair was the cutest in the universe."

It sounded like she was confusing cosmetology and cosmology.

Jill found it difficult to stifle a grin. "Did he ever visit with you and your husband?"

"No. I don't think Earl, that's my husband, I don't think Earl liked him. He could be sort of aloof, you know. I suppose that was the German in him."

"Do you know if he had many visitors?" I asked.

"Not that I know of. I'm a waitress at Olive Garden, so I work nights a lot. There was only one person I recall seeing on a few occasions. He was tall and lanky and drove a white Mustang."

She sounded like a nosy neighbor, probably watched the action down below her window.

"Did you ever see him with a lady friend?" Jill asked.

"He never brought one around here that I'm aware of. Of course, I didn't keep up with his every move."

Of course.

"When you talked to him occasionally," I said, "did he ever mention an interest in sports?"

She rested her chin on one hand and cut her eyes toward me. "He may have talked about football, like watching the Titans."

"Nothing about basketball?"

"There's no basketball court around here," she said in a bit of a huff. "Anyway, I didn't talk with him all that much. Mostly like 'how ya doin' or 'nice day for a walk.' Stuff like that."

"Did he talk any about auto racing?"

She moved her head from side to side as if to jar loose a memory. "He may have said something about going to the Superspeedway."

"Did you see him yesterday?" I asked.

"Matter of fact, I did. I'd just come back from the grocery and passed him on the stairway. He just breezed right by me like I wasn't there. Must've had his head full of something."

I leaned forward for emphasis. "Can you think of anything about Wechsel that would give us some insight into him? Something that might provide a hint as to why somebody might want to harm him?"

"Jeez. I didn't know him all that well. One thing I remember, though, he must've had a touchy temper. I heard him out in the hallway on a few occasions shouting into his phone."

"Did you hear any names?"

She rubbed her chin as she pondered the question. "Frank somebody? I don't know. With that accent, I'm not sure. It was in the last few days, I think."

![chapter ornament] **6**

WHEN WE GOT BACK to the office, I did a database search on Richard Ullery while Jill updated the case file on all we had learned today. Sometimes we pursued certain aspects of a case alone, but most of the time we counted on the synergy of working together to produce the best results. As my mother always told me, two heads are better than one, even if one is a goat's head. I was always a bit stubborn.

I had no trouble finding Arnold Wechsel's friend. There were few Ullerys in the Nashville area, and only one Richard. When I saw his employer, Nashville Superspeedway, I knew we had our man. Other data gave his age as twenty-eight, divorced, holder of an associate degree in business from Vol State Community College. I suspected he also drove a Ford Mustang. He lived in an apartment complex in Hermitage, not far from our house.

"Got him," I told Jill. "He's practically a neighbor."

"See if he's home."

He wasn't, but his answering machine gave me his cell phone number. He answered on the first ring.

"Dick Ullery?"

"Yeah. Who's this?"

"Greg McKenzie. I'm the man who was supposed to meet Arnold Wechsel last night and found him dead. I hope you can help me out."

"Man, that was a bad scene." He gave a deep sigh.

"Whoever shot him oughta get the nasty needle. Arnold was one cool dude."

"We'll have to catch the killer first. Maybe you can help. I live in Hermitage, not far from your apartment. I'd like to talk to you tonight if that's possible."

"You're a private eye, right?"

"Yes. Arnold called and asked me to meet him. Have you talked to the police?"

"No. I guess I should, but I don't need my name in the papers over some shit like this."

I was a little surprised Phil hadn't found him. Pete Lara must have held back when he talked to the detective. "Are you at the Superspeedway now?" I asked.

"Yeah, but I'll be leaving shortly. Why don't you come over around seven?"

AS SOON AS WE got home, Jill whipped up "a little something," in Jill McKenzie terms. She sautéed fresh vegetables in garlic butter prepared with her unique blend of spices, to go with tilapia filets with a parmesan-encrusted topping. The finished plate looked like something out of a gourmet restaurant kitchen. After that mini-feast, we headed over to Dick Ullery's apartment.

The entrance to the complex had been decorated in colorful flashing garlands. Spotlights bathed large foam snowmen that stood like frozen sentries at either side of the divided roadway. Wide parking areas flanked the brick and vinyl-sided buildings. We found a vacant spot among the mass of cars that included a 2002 Mustang outside Ullery's unit.

I smelled wood smoke from somebody's fireplace as I rang the bell. The man who opened the door stood a little taller than me at six feet plus. Lean as a greyhound, he had the haggard expression of a man at the end of a rough day. Must have been some mini-crisis since there were no races this time of year. We followed him inside a sparely-furnished living room. A gray sofa, a recliner, a large-screen TV, and a well-stocked bookcase with glass doors were placed seemingly at random. I suspected it was a symptom of a disorganized lifestyle. He invited us to have a seat on the sofa.

"I don't know what I can tell you," he said. "This business has bugged me all day. What could prompt somebody to do a thing like that? It makes no sense. Sure, Arnold could get a bit testy when something didn't go his way, but..." His voice petered out.

"Did he ever talk about somebody named Frank?" I asked.

"Not that I remember. Who's Frank?"

"A neighbor heard him talking on the phone to somebody named Frank. He sounded angry. Do you know of anybody he was having trouble with?"

Ullery sat with his arms leaning on slender thighs, hands gripping his knees, eyes downcast. "He didn't always agree with stuff they did at that shop where he worked. I never heard him talk about any real trouble, though."

"You work at the Superspeedway," I said. "Is that how you met him?"

His eyes flicked up toward mine. "Yeah. I'm involved in PR. Arnold came out one day wanting somebody to show him around. I was elected. We hit it off pretty good. I found it interesting this young German guy wanted to be a NASCAR crew chief."

"Is that what he was working toward?"

"Yeah. It was a long shot. Chiefs usually get there by working their way up through a pit crew." He sat up suddenly and wiped his hands across his face. "Can I get you guys something? I need a beer."

"Go ahead and get your beer," I said. "We just finished dinner. We're fine."

He took a few quick strides into the kitchen and returned with a Bud Lite.

"I had planned to take Arnold out to meet my granddad next week," Ullery said. "He lives on a farm up in Robertson County."

"What was the occasion?"

"Granddad spent time in Germany as a prisoner of war during World War II. He wanted to talk to Arnold about the way things are over there now. He'll really be disappointed to hear about this."

"Sad," I said.

Jill looked across at him. "We heard that Arnold was involved in something besides the auto shop. Was he working with a pit crew?"

Ullery took a swig of beer and set the can on the carpet beside the recliner. "He didn't work with a crew, but he'd been hanging out with guys from the Victor Block Racing Team. They're based in Nashville and race in the NASCAR Nationwide Series. Not a bad idea, actually. Given a little time, he might have gotten on the team. He knew his way around the cars for sure."

"Was he a gambler?" I asked. "The homicide detective said he had a lot of money in his billfold."

"He did a little gambling now and then. I went with him to the boat a few times. You know, Harrah's casino on the Ohio River up in Metropolis."

Jill and I made that trek up I-24 to the Illinois side of the river occasionally. We looked on it as a recreational thing and set a fairly modest limit for what we'd spend. Sometimes we came back winners. Most of the time we didn't.

"Did Arnold ever win big?" Jill asked.

"A few hundred bucks, at best. He talked about making bets a few times, but I never heard anything that sounded like he'd scored any real hits at it."

I thought about the problem a lot of players faced with borrowing to cover their bets. "Did he ever mention owing money to somebody, maybe a gambling debt?"

"Not a chance. He was a real nut about staying out of debt. I doubt he'd ever have bought a house, since he'd've had to borrow money to do it. Anyway, he was saving his money to go back to school."

"Did he have any lady friends?" Jill asked.

"He might have, but he didn't talk about it. Arnold was the most private guy I've ever met. He wasn't real outgoing, didn't make friends easily, but he was sharp as a filet knife."

"That's sharp," Jill said with a gourmet grin.

"Do you know if he was working anywhere besides the race car shop?" I asked. "Another job might account for the extra money."

Ullery took a gulp of his beer. "He was doing something for some guy, but I'm not sure who or what. He didn't like people nosing into his business, so I didn't ask a lot of questions."

"Did he talk about this extra job at all?"

"Y'know, it's funny, as shy as he was. He actually seemed to enjoy meeting people he never expected to meet and going places he never expected to go. He talked about that a bit, although he never said exactly what he was doing."

"What sort of people and places?"

"As I say, he was a little short on details, but he mentioned once meeting an exec at a big hospital chain. The guy lived in a fancy house in Belle Meade. He talked about some others, but the only one I remember him mentioning by name was this

Freddie Ford, the car dealer you see all over TV. Arnold said he was a real oddball."

"When was the last time you saw Arnold?" I asked.

He looked thoughtful. "Would've been Friday afternoon. I was off and we met for a beer."

"Was he in a good mood?"

Ullery stretched his fingers out and wiggled his hands in a gesture of uncertainty. "Mood was a hard thing to pin down with Arnold. He could be up when you thought he was down, and vice versa."

"So how did he seem Friday afternoon?"

"Like something was bothering him, but he didn't want to talk about it. He would grin and try to act silly, but his heart wasn't in it." He shook his head. "I hate this. I loved him like a brother."

A long driveway through the woods led to our house. After a dogleg to the right, the hard-packed gravel ended at a large log structure that sat in the midst of a cleared area. The mailbox on the street showed only our house number, but anyone with basic computer smarts could find out who lived at that address. I no longer worried about it, though when we first moved in I wanted to remain anonymous in case some of the felons I helped put in prison should come looking for me. Now that we were established in the PI business, anybody interested in tracking me down could find the office number in the phone book, but the home number was unlisted. That was no guarantee of anonymity.

I think the original owner of the property had visions of living on a ranch. Wooden gateposts and short pseudo fences stood at the entrance to the driveway. I started turning in at our mailbox when I spotted a car parked at the side of the street, facing us, forty to fifty yards ahead. It wasn't something we normally saw along here. People usually parked in driveways. I had a bad feeling about it. I swung back into the street and drove on toward the car.

"What are you—?"

"Try to get a license number when we pass that car," I said.

I slowed as we approached a large, dark-colored SUV. As we came closer, the vehicle lunged forward and sped into the night without any lights.

"It's too dark to see the tag number," Jill shouted, looking back, her voice laced with frustration.

My Jeep Cherokee did not enjoy the same tight turning radius of Jill's Toyota Camry. I swung into our neighbors' driveway, reversed directions, and headed back down the street. By that time, the SUV was already out of sight around a curve.

I raced to the curve, then slowed. Nothing but a string of darkened houses on either side of a vacant street. No cars. With the lead he had on us, there were too many opportunities to turn in or take a side street. I had lost him. I drove to the next intersection, grumbled silently, did a U-turn, and headed home.

 7

SHORTLY AFTER WE SWUNG into the clearing beyond the woods, motion-activated floodlights bathed the house in a glow bright enough to reveal every knothole in the logs. I looked around but saw nothing amiss. Activating the opener, I pulled into the garage and closed the door behind us. We had keyless entry pads on all the outside entrances, including the one from the garage into the house. I punched in the current code and opened the door for Jill.

"Who do you suppose it was?" she asked. She had remained quiet as a rag doll on the way back home.

"He didn't intend for us to find out." I hung my jacket in the hall closet beside her fur-collared coat.

"Do you know anybody who drives a black Cadillac Escalade?"

Though the night was dark and the visibility poor, the vehicle was obviously a luxury SUV and we'd agreed that was most likely the model.

"I can't think of anybody who drives an Escalade of any color," I said. "But I'd sure as hell like to know who this one was."

She gave me a beady eye. My wife has never learned to appreciate my four-letter vocabulary, which is why I use it sparingly. I followed her into the large country kitchen, her favorite part of the house, and sat at the round maple table that matched the cabinets.

Jill leaned against the counter. "Do you think he was watching for us?"

"He was certainly up to no good. Why else would he leave in such a hurry? And without lights."

"What should we do about it?"

"We're going to keep a careful eye out for anything else that doesn't match the ordinary. And we'll be armed like pirates whenever we go out until this case is solved."

She poured water into the coffee maker. "Then you think this has something to do with Terry Tremont's case."

"What else could it be? Either that or Arnold Wechsel's murder, which are probably one and the same."

She spooned in Columbian coffee, pressed the switch, turned, and grinned. "Armed like pirates, huh? That means armed to the teeth. Do I have to go around with a knife in my mouth?"

Jill was not the type to cave in at the prospect of danger. She had faced down more than a few crises at the controls of an airplane. She accepted that a potential menace should be respected but not dreaded. She had also bought into my practice of countering intimidation by finding a way to laugh at it.

"The knife is optional," I said. "But carry that little .38 in your bra."

I said it as a joke, but what I had begun to feel was far from amusement. I drummed my fingers on the table. "Having said that, I'll have to admit I don't like this one bit."

"Could Phil help us?"

"I'm afraid Phil doesn't have time to check out every Escalade owner in Metro and surrounding counties. But I need to tip him off about Dick Ullery."

When I got Detective Adamson on the phone, I gave him a friendly needle prick. "Did I disturb your nap again?"

"Big joke. I haven't been home long enough to stretch my arms, much less stretch out on a recliner. If you're fishing for new developments, you've cast your line in the wrong stream, buddy. There ain't any."

"Maybe I can help out," I said. "Have you come across the name Dick Ullery?"

"Damn, Greg. I should've known you'd outflank us." He sounded a bit miffed. "Ullery's name turned up this afternoon. We haven't checked him out yet. What do you know about him?"

"Jill and I just came from his apartment. It's not far from our house."

I told him what we had learned from the Superspeedway employee.

"I suppose I should talk to the chief and see if I can't deputize you to join my team on this."

"Not a bad idea. If Arnold's murder turns out to be unrelated to our case, I'm not sure Terry Tremont will pay our bill. Do I get overtime?"

"Ha! They tell us to close our cases in double-time. Forget the overtime."

Jill brought my coffee over and set it on the table.

"Be glad you're not in the military," I said. "We were on duty twenty-four/seven at the designated pay rate."

"Yeah, it's tough all over. Thanks for the tip, though. For your information, the ME is releasing the body. They're supposed to contact the family about sending him back to Germany."

"What did the autopsy show?"

"One interesting point. This isn't general knowledge, so keep it under your Titan's cap. As you know, he was shot at close range through the cheek. The bullet had an upward trajectory. It was a hollow-point nine millimeter. The TBI lab is running tests on it."

That meant the bullet would give up any secrets it held. The firearms section of the Tennessee Bureau of Investigation Forensics Lab did great work. I wasn't through with Phil yet, though. I took a sip of coffee and told him about the Cadillac SUV lurking on our street.

"What the hell," he said after hearing my story. "You think it's related to Wechsel's murder?"

"If it isn't, I have no idea what it could mean. We don't have any other cases that would warrant something weird like this."

"I've heard you talk about the possibility of some old case from your Air Force days coming back to haunt you."

"That's always a possibility. I've worked some grisly cases, but nobody's threatened me in years."

"Want me to ask Patrol to keep an eye on your place?"

"It couldn't hurt, but I don't know that it would help, either."

"I'll pass the word along. Let me know if anything else happens."

8

I AWOKE THE NEXT morning to an icy north wind rattling the windows. The deck of surly clouds looked low enough to reach out and grab a handful. The forecast called for temperatures to hover below the freezing mark, which meant we'd be traipsing about like Eskimos. Jill wasn't the best morning person, particularly on a frigid day like this, but I managed to coax her out of bed with the smell of hot coffee. Jeff Price called from Ramstein Air Base while we were eating breakfast.

"I hope it isn't too early for you," he said. "It's afternoon over here."

I glanced at Jill, whose eyes still looked like they'd been raised to only half-staff. "We've been up for a while. Did your wife get word they've released Arnold's body?"

"They contacted her sister. I think they're flying him back here tomorrow. Have you come up with any information?"

I told him what I could about our investigation so far. "What about you?" I asked. "Learn anything additional about Arnold that might be helpful?"

"His mother said she's really been worried the past couple of months. He talked about all this 'easy money' he'd been making. She knew he liked to bet on things before he left here, but he denied gambling in the States. I didn't tell her otherwise. Still, she had a feeling this new job was somehow related to it."

I thought about what Dick Ullery had said regarding people Arnold had met. Could they be involved with gambling?

When we were ready to leave for work, Jill eyed the kitchen clock. "We'd better skip the office if we're going to make it out West End for our eight-thirty appointment with Bradley Smotherman. Rush hour isn't over yet."

I agreed. You never knew what you'd run into on I-40. It was like playing Russian roulette, hoping to click on an empty lane. Our office was near the longest entrance ramp to the interstate I'd ever encountered. It must have been more than a mile long. I-40 would take us downtown to the Broadway exit and a short drive out to Smotherman's office. But with the morning rush, all bets were off.

I didn't have any real concern that we might encounter a problem this morning, but I wasn't taking any chances, either. I holstered my 9mm Sig-Sauer P-229 before we hit the road. As it turned out, despite five lanes of traffic, a rear-end collision near the airport slowed us to the point that we made our appointment with only minutes to spare. I didn't envy the cops who stood in the icy wind, arms waving in an attempt to keep traffic from stalling, which it did anyway. Maybe they were just moving to keep from freezing. I'd worked in a hell of a lot worse conditions. I served a tour at a base in Minot, North Dakota where the average temperature in December was minus thirteen degrees. Nashville hadn't seen a snowflake this month, though the dark folds of cloud jammed together overhead looked capable of producing a flurry or two.

We had just passed where West End split off from Broadway when a red light caught us. I turned to ask Jill if I needed to adjust the heater and my gaze hit on the driver of a pickup truck in the next lane. He had a sharp, angular face, with a chin that seemed almost pointed. I did a double take.

The man looked around at me and grinned. Then the light changed, and he took off.

Jill saw my frown and asked, "What's wrong? The light's changed. Let's go."

I gunned the Jeep, keeping the truck in view. It was a light blue Ford F-150. I couldn't see the license plate. Solid traffic in the right lane prevented my getting behind him. I pounded the steering wheel angrily as he turned off West End at the next intersection. There was no way I could follow him.

Jill leaned toward me. "What's going on, Greg?"

"Izzy Isabell was driving that truck," I said. "I'd swear to it." I recalled the last time I saw him, being led out of the courtroom in handcuffs.

"Is that the navigator you arrested on drug charges?"

"Right. It was back in the late eighties. While he was in jail, he talked about arranging the murder of some witnesses, including me. He was real unhappy that I caught him in the first place."

"Was he from Nashville?" Jill asked.

"No. Louisville."

"Are you sure that was him in the truck?"

"He has a face I could never forget, even with a little age on it. And he grinned when he looked at me. He obviously knew who I was. It's possible he was following us."

"If he's out of prison, shouldn't Colonel Grigsby have called you?"

"I need to check with him and find out what's happened."

My former OSI commander, the colonel kept tabs on the whereabouts of incorrigible criminals we had put away. He advised us when somebody who didn't have our best interests at heart got put back on the streets. That included Izzy Isabell, a name his parents had given him for Lord knows why. The lieutenant, a navigator on a KC-135 Stratotanker, always carried a heavy briefcase for his maps and charts and whatever else he required to get the tanker to its rendezvous with jets that needed air-to-air refueling. I finally got proof that it had also contained bricks of cocaine.

IF ANYONE DOUBTED Bradley Smotherman's addiction to ice hockey, the sign on his office suite provided the unequivocal answer—Hatrick Brake Company. A "hat trick," of course, was when one player scored three goals in a game. Terry Tremont had told us that Smotherman grew up in Rochester, New York, one of the original hotbeds of pro hockey. His company manufactured disc brake assemblies. He relocated here when Nissan's arrival made Middle Tennessee a favorite spot to build new auto plants and make parts that went into the assembly of cars.

Besides all the jungle-like greenery of contemporary office décor, the reception area featured a mock-up of the driver side of a sports car with the wheels missing to show the brake assembly. Two bright-eyed young blondes occupied desks shaped like they'd been designed by someone with a scroll saw and a free-form mindset. I handed the nearest one my business card.

"Greg and Jill McKenzie," I said with my best PR smile. "We have an appointment with Mr. Smotherman."

She glanced at a sheet on her desk and returned my smile with one straight off a tooth-whitening commercial. "Please have a seat. He'll be right with you."

She spoke on the phone as we took our seats in softly upholstered earth-toned chairs. Looking around, I saw the Predators' influence in hockey posters and paintings on the walls. We had just settled in when the receptionist's phone rang. She turned to the other girl, who'd have made a great model for *Sports Illustrated*'s swimsuit issue.

"Dolores, take Mr. and Mrs. McKenzie back to Mr. Smotherman's office."

As we followed Dolores through a door to a long hallway, the hockey motif jumped out at us. Wallpaper up to chair rail height featured a succession of hockey sticks, pucks, skates, helmets, and other items peculiar to the sport. I was forced to admit, Bradley Smotherman had to be the quintessential fan.

He met us at the door and ushered us to an area at one side of the ample office where several chairs were arranged around a low walnut coffee table. The walls sported framed hockey scenes.

"Welcome to Hatrick," he said in his clipped New York accent.

I had dressed in my best new-client outfit, white shirt and tie, dark blue blazer. Jill looked stylish as usual in a burgundy suit. But our host, with ruddy cheeks and short brown hair, could have just stepped out of a hockey arena suite. Decked out in black slacks and an open-collared white knit shirt emblazoned with the Pred's sabretooth tiger logo, he looked early fifties.

"Please have a seat," he said, moving to one of the chairs. "Would you like coffee or a Coke?"

Jill shook her head.

"Thanks, we're fine," I said. I let my gaze sweep around the office. "You must be quite a hockey fan, Mr. Smotherman."

He feigned a frown, then laughed. "Now where did you get that idea?"

"I'm sure Terry Tremont gave you some background on us," I said, bypassing the small talk. "We'd like to know the circumstances that led to our being brought in."

"Fair enough. I understand you're retired Air Force. I was a Navy pilot after college. Trained at Pensacola."

Jill's eyes brightened. "We have...make that *had* a condo

on Perdido Key, before the hurricane turned it inside out a few months ago. We always watched the Blue Angels practice when we were down there."

"Sorry to hear about your condo. I wasn't quite good enough for the Blue Angels. I did my share of low-level buzzing, though. That was back in my younger days." Smotherman chuckled, then abruptly switched the topic. "How familiar are you with the effort to bring a National Basketball Association team to Nashville?"

"I've read some of the newspaper accounts and heard a bit on TV," I said.

"Then you probably know of the attempt back in 2001 to bring the Grizzlies here from Vancouver. We opposed it, but the idea never got past the talk stage before they decided to move the team to Memphis. This effort is more dedicated. The front man for the deal is a smooth-talker named Louie Aregis. He's a venture capitalist who recently moved his investment company here from, would you believe, Pensacola?"

"We saw the name," Jill said. "We didn't recognize it."

"I'm told he has plenty of cash," Smotherman said. "And he has some well-heeled partners in Howard Hays and Fred Ricketts."

I noted his easy manner of speaking, the mark of a man who was sure of himself.

"I know Hays heads the Dollar Deal retail store chain," I said. "He's in the news frequently. Who is Ricketts?"

The Hatrick president folded his arms. "He runs a company in Brentwood that designs software for medical practices. Their group proposes to use the Preds' arena for basketball. It would take a lot of coordination between hockey and basketball schedules, but that's not the main problem. The fan base here will support two professional teams. Three...I don't think so."

"You're afraid it would cause the Predators to fail," I said.

"Likely both teams would fail."

"Okay. I see your problem. So you're creating a campaign to discourage support for the basketball franchise?"

"That's the basic idea. We've hired a PR firm to convince the public and the city fathers that it wouldn't be the best thing for Nashville. Gordon Franklin and Mack Nolan joined me in putting up money for the project."

"We're supposed to see Franklin at eleven-thirty. I understand he's a CPA."

"A very competent CPA. He lives and breathes number crunching. I suspect his boxers have dollar signs on them. If anything happened to that accounting practice, he'd be ready for the grave."

"How did he get interested in hockey?" I asked.

"I'm not sure, but it's the only thing I've seen that makes him blossom out. He's a bachelor and a very private person. Don't be surprised if he seems a bit terse. I guess an outgoing personality isn't a requirement for being a CPA."

"We haven't been able to get an appointment with Mack Nolan," Jill said.

"He's a fast-moving young guy at the top of his form. Ice hockey is something of a passion for him. I think it's a way to let off steam from the hectic pace he keeps between public appearances, recording sessions, and whatever else he does. It's sure better than popping pills like so many of them do. You may have to corner him at a Pred's game."

"What about this rumor thing Terry Tremont mentioned?" I asked.

Smotherman leaned his elbows on the desk, striking a thoughtful pose. "It was Mack who received a report that something may not be kosher about the NBA deal. Terry suggested bringing you in to check into it."

I glanced at Jill and caught her brows going up.

"Have you ever heard of an Arnold Wechsel, Mr. Smotherman?" I asked.

He gave me a blank stare as he pondered the name. "No. Not that I can recall."

"Did you see the story in the morning paper yesterday about a murder at an auto repair shop in the Dickerson Pike area?"

He leaned back in the chair and laced his fingers. "I saw the headline but didn't read the story. That is an area I'm not familiar with."

I wasn't surprised, but I told him about the phone call from Wechsel and that I was the one who found the body.

"My, God!" His eyes narrowed, and his face took on a pinched look. "He said it would blow your mind?"

"Words to that effect. I have no idea what he was talking about. It's possible, perhaps probable, the murder had some connection. We just don't know at this point."

He cocked his head to one side and spoke persuasively. "This could be the tip of the iceberg we've been hoping to find."

"The question is who knew we had been hired besides Terry Tremont and you? How did Arnold Wechsel know about us?"

Smotherman's brow wrinkled. "I called both Franklin and Nolan."

"Did you talk to Nolan?"

"No. I left word with his manager."

"That would be Mr. Oakley?" Jill asked.

"Right."

"Did you tell him about us?"

"Yes. I told him you'd been retained by Terry to assist us, but I didn't say exactly why. I asked him to have Mack call me."

I thought about that for a moment. "Did he?"

"Not until late last night. He was in California."

"And you told no one else?"

He cocked his head thoughtfully. "Only my secretary."

I challenged him with the same request I had given Terry Tremont, that he make sure his secretary had not passed the information on to others.

"What do you plan to do next?" he asked.

"It looks like we're back to basic detective work," I said.

Jill opened her handbag, took out a small notebook and began jotting notes on it. "We'll need full backgrounds on Howard Hays and Fred Ricketts," she said. "In addition to Louie Aregis."

"I have a good contact in Metro Homicide who should be able to provide some help with the murder of Arnold Wechsel. Which brings up the point of confidentiality. Is it necessary that our relationship to Protect Our Preds remain private?"

Smotherman frowned. "We'd prefer the other side didn't know we're looking into their operation. Total secrecy is impossible, of course. Just avoid connecting us with your investigation."

"Okay," I said. "We'll work as quietly as possible."

 **9**

BACK AT THE OFFICE, Jill got out our large travel cups, heated water, and shoveled in spoonfuls of cappuccino mix, our favorite beverage. McKenzie Investigations occupied a small nook in the strip center, its broad front window artfully painted with a scene from the Gardens at Versailles. The yellow, white and purple blossoms contrasted sharply with the reds and greens of Christmas decorations that dominated the stores on either side of us.

Before we huddled around my desk for a strategy session, I called Colonel Grigsby at Andrews Air Force Base. I asked him if Lieutenant Isabell had been released from prison.

"He's one of those I'm supposed to be informed about," the colonel said, "but I haven't heard anything. I'll check into it and give you a call."

When I got off the phone, Jill sat at the table with our cappuccino cups.

"Grigsby doesn't know anything," I said. "He'll let me know. Got your notes ready?"

"Who do we start with?"

"Let's start at the top."

"That would be Mr. Louie Aregis, the investment fellow. His company is Coastal Capital Ventures. Since the Cumberland River provides the closest thing we have to a coast, maybe he should change it to Riverfront Capital Ventures."

"I think Brad Smotherman would be happy to see him go

back to the Gulf Coast. Let's check him out with a database search. Why don't you get onto that? I'll see if I can track down Red Tarkington."

"The NCIS agent in Pensacola who helped us down there last year?" Jill asked.

"Right. Last time I talked to Ted Kennerly, he said Red spoke of getting out of the Navy and taking a shot at the PI business in Florida."

Ted was a former OSI protégé currently the Special Agent in Charge at Arnold Air Force Base south of Nashville. We had kept in touch over the years. I'd used him on occasion to get info from places he had privy to but I didn't. Tarkington worked with us some years back on a joint-service case at Pearl Harbor and became close friends with Ted. They communicated frequently by phone and email.

I reached Ted at his office. "Have you heard anything more from Red Tarkington about hanging up his sailor hat and becoming a PI?" I asked.

"Sure have, Boss. He's already out of the service."

Ted still used the "Boss" nickname I had when I was his Special Agent in Charge. "When did it happen?"

"About a month ago. He was working on getting a private investigator license. I understood he plans to set up shop in Pensacola. The way things are down there, I imagine there's lots of opportunity for fraud in reconstruction. Probably a good climate for an investigator. What's going on? Jill hasn't resigned as your partner, has she?"

Ted and Jill had a special relationship after she flew him to Boston to be with his dying mother when he couldn't get there by commercial air.

"Nothing like that," I said. "We have a new case that involves a man who recently moved his business here from the Panhandle."

"I bet Red could help you out. Hold a sec and I'll get you his phone number."

I wrote down the number, sent regards to Ted's wife, Karen, and hung up. Jill was still digging around on the Internet.

"Come up with anything yet?" I asked.

"I'm checking a couple of sources. Looks like there's no shortage of info on Aregis out there."

I went back to the phone and punched in Red Tarkington's number.

"This is Greg McKenzie," I said when he answered.

"Hi, Colonel. I was asking Ted about you recently. He said you folks had solved another murder up there. Are you branching out into homicide?"

"Hardly," I said with a chuckle. "Right now we're doing an investigation that's linked to a guy who moved his firm here from Pensacola a few months ago. Ted said you planned to get into the PI business. That true?"

"I'm working on getting set up. Got my license. Ready to rent an office and line up some clients."

"We'd like to be your first, Red. We need you to look around down there for anything that might appear questionable about one Louie Aregis or his company, Coastal Capital Ventures."

After getting Red onboard, I recalled that he had been a civilian cop before joining the military, serving in the Louisville, Kentucky Police Department. I told him about Izzy Isabell.

"I may need to talk to somebody up there," I said. "Do you still have any contacts?"

"Call Lt. Bob Dobyns." He spelled the name for me. "Bob is in the Criminal Intelligence Unit."

I had just gotten off the phone when a visitor arrived. We didn't get a lot of walk-ins in our out-of-the-way location, and this one hardly bore the look of a prospective client. After stepping through the door, he hesitated, shifted his bleary eyes about, and approached my desk. Beneath a brown fedora that looked like it had been twisted into a cylinder a few times, he wore a gray sweat shirt, over that a long black coat. The tail of the coat had evidently been snagged on a nail. From his appearance, he might have been a down-and-out PI from an old pulp novel. He had a bristly beard and his hands showed no sign of having been introduced to soap lately.

"You Greg McKenzie?" he asked.

I nodded. "What can I do for you?"

"I have some information you need." His voice was scratchy, like a well-worn 78 rpm record.

"What makes you think I need it?"

"It'll cost you to find out."

I had been exposed to enough pseudo-snitch winos to be a confirmed skeptic. I stood and faced him. He was a couple of inches shorter than me. "You'll have to do better than that if you want any of our money."

"It's about that shootin' Saturday night."

Now he had my attention. "How does it involve the shooting?"

"How?"

"Yeah, what do you know that's worth my giving you any cash to find out? Do you know who fired the shot?"

"Maybe."

"Did you see the shooter?"

"I heard him shoot and saw him run out to his car."

"What kind of car did he drive?"

"Now we're talking cash." He grinned, showing a couple of missing teeth.

"Tell me the make of the car and a license number and I'll give you twenty bucks."

His reddened eyes flared like Roman candles about to fire. He jammed his fists against spindly hips. "Twenty! You think I'm some idgit asshole? You know how much it cost me to ride a bus out here? Make it a hunnert."

I checked him out a little more closely. He was nobody's fool. "Why did you come here instead of to the cops?"

"I don't like cops. They're nothin' but trouble."

"How do I know you aren't just making this up?"

"Gimme fifty now and the other fifty when you check it out."

I had to admire his tenacity, but I wasn't about to put out that kind of money on faith alone. "How would I find you if I came looking?"

"I hang out around Dickerson Pike and Trinity Lane. Just ask for Fingers."

I wondered if that nickname had come from a habit of picking pockets or doing a little shoplifting. "Tell me somebody out there who'd know you."

He looked down, obviously scratching about for an answer. "Tommy at A and R Café. He gives me a cup of coffee now and then."

I reached down and flipped through my phone book to the café's listing. I called the number and asked for Tommy.

"You're talking to him," a lively voice said.

"I have a guy here who goes by the name of Fingers," I said. "He tells me you know him."

"Afraid so. He's harmless, though. Always hanging around the area. He trying to talk you out of some money?"

"A little business deal. He wants to sell me some information. Is he believable?"

Tommy paused a moment. "My caller ID shows McKenzie Investigations. Are you the man who found that body over here Saturday night?"

I looked across at Fingers and wondered what was coming. "Right."

"I guess I'm responsible. I gave him your name."

"How'd that happen?"

"He asked me if there was something in the newspaper Sunday about a shooting around here the night before. I read the story to him—he's not too good at reading. He wanted to know where your office was and I told him. I had no idea he'd go out there."

"He rode the bus," I said. "Sounds like he might be legitimate, doesn't it. Do you think I could find him over there if I came looking?"

"Long as you don't plan to make him rich. I know where he sleeps when it doesn't get too far below freezing."

I thanked him and hung up. I pulled out my billfold and counted out two twenties and a ten. I laid them on the desk but kept my hand on them.

"The information, please," I said.

He took a scrap of paper from his coat pocket and tossed it on my desk. It had the three-letter, three-number combination found on Tennessee license plates.

"What kind of car?" I asked.

"One of them big sport utility trucks. Black. Not sure what make. It was too dark."

"Where were you when you saw it?"

"In front of the building next to the repair shop. His truck was parked on the street."

"Could you identify the man?"

"Naw. I didn't get a good look at him. Didn't look too big, though, even bundled up in that wind."

"But you're sure of this number?"

"Sure as my name's Fingers O'Malley."

I pushed the bills toward him. He grabbed them and

hurried out the door. I picked up the phone and called Phil Adamson.

"You did what?" he said when I told him about Fingers.

"I paid him fifty bucks for the license number of Arnold Wechsel's killer. Sounded like the SUV we saw on the street last night."

I read off the tag number.

"Hold on and let me check it out." I listened to muffled office noises for a couple of minutes until Phil came back. "Hang on while I check one more thing."

After another two or three minutes, he said, "My friend, you just got snookered. That number is registered to a yellow Volkswagen Beetle. Hardly what I'd call a big black SUV."

"Maybe the plate was stolen from the VW," I said.

"I called the owner. She's a retired schoolteacher who confirmed the plate is still on her Volkswagen."

10

WHEN I TOLD JILL what Phil had found, she just shook her head. I walked over to where she stood beside the printer. It whirred away, spitting out a succession of sheets from her data search on Louie Aregis.

"I still think Fingers O'Malley saw something that night," I said.

"He sure as heck saw that fifty dollars on your desk."

Okay, so I took a gamble and it appeared that I lost. I'd deal with Mr. O'Malley later. I pointed at the paper tray. "Find some interesting stuff?"

"You be the judge."

She handed me the first page. Aregis was born in 1969 in Orlando, Florida, where his father was employed at the developing project that would become known as Disney World. He grew up in the Orlando area. After graduating from Florida State University in Tallahassee with a degree in finance, he took a position with a brokerage firm there and married his college sweetheart, a Pensacola girl. Three years later, the family moved to Florida's westernmost city where Louie went to work for Coastal Capital Ventures, the firm owned by his wife's father. Aregis took over the business four years ago after his father-in-law's death.

"Looks like he married well," I said.

"Reminds me of the way they talked about Nashville in my younger days," Jill said. "It was called 'The Son-in-Law Town.'

Young Vanderbilt graduates married the daughters of wealthy businessmen, then moved up to cushy jobs."

A St. Louis native, I knew little about Nashville prior to moving here. My only connection had been a tour of duty at the former Sewart Air Force Base in Smyrna, just south of the city. That was my first OSI assignment, which provided me the opportunity to meet Jill, a college student in the aviation program at nearby Middle Tennessee State.

When she spread the sheets from the data search across her desk, she pulled out one and handed it to me. "This is something you might want to dig into a little more deeply."

It included a reference to a Tallahassee newspaper story from Aregis' college days. Nineteen at the time, he was involved in a shooting incident at his fraternity house at Florida State. According to the story, he shot a fraternity brother in the arm with a .38 caliber revolver. There were conflicting accounts from witnesses about an argument, but both he and the victim described it as an accident. Aregis said they were horsing around with the gun when it discharged. He told police he had found the weapon in a clump of bushes behind the house. A later story said authorities traced the revolver to a Miami man who had reported it stolen a few years earlier. The university disciplined both boys and no charges were filed.

I skimmed through the other pages Jill had printed but saw nothing that jumped out at me. I decided to save it for later.

"Let's split up the other two NBA investors and do searches on them," I said.

"Okay, I'll take the easy one. Everybody knows Howard Hays. See what you can dig up on Fred Ricketts."

"I thought the senior investigator got first choice," I said.

"If the senior investigator wants something besides leftovers for dinner, he'd better get busy on Mr. Ricketts."

I should have known better. In a battle of wits, I always got the nit. I turned to my computer and fired up a database search. I soon learned that Ricketts was owner of Physicians and Surgeons Software, Inc., better known as P&S Software. Originally from Indianapolis, he had been in upper management with one of Nashville's major hospital chains before striking out on his own. The firm was headquartered in Brentwood, which bordered Nashville on the south and was home to many medical-related companies. According to supposedly reliable reports, Ricketts planned to take P&S public soon, giving him millions to devote to new projects, like an NBA team. One interesting side item said he was part-owner of an IndyCar racing team.

I found a magazine article about him that painted a picture of a young entrepreneur with a fiery determination to make it big. He had used the knowledge he gained at the hospital firm to create software programs that made life easier for both hospitals and medical practices. He hired the right mix of program developers and marketing pros to quickly build P&S Software into a formidable company.

Jill and I compared notes. Hays, as we knew, headed the Dollar Deal chain of small retail stores specializing in "everything for a dollar." He was big in charitable work, served on several corporate boards as well as one of the mayor's commissions, and owned a piece of a minor league baseball team in another city.

"Looks like these two are pretty reputable business types," Jill said. "I'd say we need to concentrate first on Mr. Aregis."

"Agreed. We can't hit him head-on, though. We'll have to nibble around the edges."

"Do you want to try the magazine gimmick?"

It was something we'd used before. I would pose as a magazine writer and interview the subject for a background piece. "Might work. He's fairly new in town. He won't likely know me."

"What about that picture of you Wes Knight put in the paper after the Marathon case?"

Notoriety wasn't always a good thing. "You have a point. I guess that leaves it up to you, babe. Think you can handle it?"

She gave me a few bars from *Annie Get Your Gun.* "Anything you can do I can do better."

"Okay, it's all yours."

She called Coastal Capital Ventures on her cell phone, which didn't show her name, and identified herself as a contributing writer for *Sporting World Magazine.* It sounded close enough to the real thing to fool most people. She gave me the high sign, meaning they were putting her through to Louie Aregis.

I got on the office phone and called Channel 4, the local NBC affiliate, asked to speak to the sports director, Rod Jenson. On hearing the mellow voice I associated with a square-jawed smiling face on the nightly news, I introduced myself and asked if we might get an appointment to chat with him for a few minutes.

"We have a client with an interest in the professional sports scene," I said. "I hoped you might be able to give us a little background on how things work."

"Sure. Be happy to help anyway I can."

He wouldn't have time for us today but agreed to a meeting tomorrow.

Jill looked across from her desk as I put down the phone. "Worked like a charm," she said. "I'm interviewing Aregis at nine o'clock in the morning."

"We need to craft some questions that sound innocuous but might give us an insight into what's going on with this deal," I said.

"You're the interrogator. Tell me what to ask and I'll make notes."

"Let's save that for tonight. I need to run over to the spy shop and pick up our surveillance gear. Sarge said he'd have it all ready this morning."

We had a tricky surveillance job coming up next week, and I had ordered a bunch of new equipment the fee would pay for. The small store was located on Lebanon Road not far from our office.

"Don't tarry," Jill said. "We need to leave soon for our interview with Gordon Franklin."

I cut through Andrew Jackson Parkway and made it in no more than five minutes. The sign over the door of the shop said Covert Security. I had run across the place a few months back while looking for a small, unobtrusive camera. The owner, a retired Special Forces master sergeant, looked up when I walked in.

"Hey, Colonel. Got all your stuff right here," he said, showing his usual lop-sided grin. He was a little shorter than me but with bulging, muscular arms. He wore a baseball cap with SOX across the front.

"Morning, Sarge," I said. "I didn't know you were a Chicago fan."

"Just trying out my newest gadget." He pulled off the cap and turned it upside down. "This little jewel is a camera and video recorder. Holds up to four hours. The lens looks out through the O in SOX. Neat, huh?"

I looked it over. "They get stuff any smaller and you can hide it in your eye teeth."

He chuckled. "I think the CIA already does that."

He spread the McKenzie Investigations equipment on the counter: a keychain voice recorder/transmitter, a small receiver that would fit in your pocket, a receiver that hooked over your ear like a Bluetooth phone, and a ballpoint pen voice recorder.

"They've all got instructions with them," Sarge said. "Let me know if you have any problems."

I gathered up all our surveillance goodies and headed back to the office. When I got there, Jill handed me a slip of paper.

"Colonel Grigsby, wants you to call him," she said.

When I reached my old commander, I got the news I expected.

"You're still sharp as ever, Greg," he said. "That must have been Izzy you saw. They told me he was released last week, presumably headed back to Louisville."

"He got fifteen years, didn't he?" I couldn't remember all the crooks I'd sent up, but this was one of those special cases.

"Right, for transporting and selling cocaine, assault, conspiracy to commit murder, and a variety of other charges. And I'm sure you recall how unhappy he was that you nailed him. They should have notified me the moment they turned him loose."

"Thanks. Did you get any info about his prison record?"

"Not good. He was a troublemaker. They said he associated with other former drug dealers. I suspect he'll be right back into it."

"Too bad," I said. "He was a smart operator."

"Right," Colonel Grigsby said. "You'd better watch your backside."

11

I TOLD JILL what I had learned about Izzy Isabell. She got up from her desk, stared at me, folded her arms, and asked, "Could that have been him lurking around on our street last night?"

"I hardly think so. I wouldn't expect Izzy to be driving an expensive SUV."

She leaned against the desk. "If I remember correctly, you were never able to find what he'd done with his money."

"He did a good job of hiding it, all right. What took us so long to find him was he didn't live beyond the lifestyle of a young lieutenant. If it's been waiting for him all these years, he should have plenty of cash to spend. But he was driving a Ford pickup when I saw him. I'd say that's more his speed."

"Well, I don't like the idea of his being in Nashville."

Neither did I, and I knew what I needed to do as soon as we got back from our visit with Gordon Franklin.

THE ACCOUNTING FIRM of Franklin, Gretchen and Silverman occupied a lavish suite in a suburban office building. Lavish in terms of size, not in demeanor. The dark-paneled walls, mahogany desks and subdued lighting rivaled the staid look of an old bank lobby. I'd always heard that number crunchers were a conservative lot.

A prim, white-haired secretary ushered Jill and me into a large room with all the pizzaz of the offices I had occupied in the Air Force. A signed photo of the Republican president and a few patriotic pictures adorned the walls, such as the Statue of Liberty and the flag-raising on Mount Suribachi. Unlike my typical clutter, the dark wood desk held neat stacks of spreadsheets. A paperweight atop one consisted of a small wood block emblazoned with a round symbol that appeared to be a globe bearing "MARS" in large letters. The first thing to come to mind was NASA's program to continue exploration of the red planet. I'd recently read about plans to launch a Mars Reconnaissance Orbiter next year. I wondered what connection Franklin might have to NASA.

He stood behind his desk, a short, stocky man dressed in a gray business suit with a red, white, and blue-striped tie. A neatly folded kerchief protruded from the breast pocket. I had seen my share of dull expressions, but this one was a classic. As Brad Smotherman had suggested, I suspected he found little of interest beyond those neat rows of figures on a sheet of paper. Except for ice hockey, of course. He walked with a slight limp as he came around to shake hands.

"Nice to meet you," Franklin said, though it seemed only a formality. "I understand you've already talked to Brad Smotherman."

"We have," I said. "He filled us in on the background, but we thought it best to see if you might be able to add anything."

"Have a seat." He indicated straight-backed wooden chairs in front of his desk. "I'm not sure I have anything to add, though."

After being seated, I looked across at him. "I was hoping you might know something about Arnold Wechsel."

His eyes widened. "Wechsel? Wasn't that the young man you found at that garage? I'd never heard of him until Brad told me about it yesterday. I read the story in the newspaper. I thought you probably knew him."

"I did know him, but I wasn't aware that he had any

connection to this NBA deal, other than what he said when he asked me to meet him."

"Didn't he say why he wanted to talk to you?"

"No specifics. I suspect it involved those rumors Bradley Smotherman mentioned. Have you heard anything along that line? A hint of something shifty that might be going on?"

"Sorry." He shook his head. "I don't travel in the same circles as Brad and Mack. I wasn't privy to any of that stuff."

"Are you familiar with the three men who are spearheading the effort, Louie Aregis, Howard Hays, and Fred Ricketts?"

"I don't know any of them personally. I'm familiar with their reputations, except for this Aregis fellow. He's new around town."

"What sort of things is Protect Our Preds cooking up to counter the threat from the basketball competition?"

He gave a brief shake of his head. "I left all that up to Brad and Mack. I agreed to help out with the financing, but with tax season coming up, I'm too busy to get involved in all those details."

"As an accountant, you must have some idea of how an NBA team would affect the Predators financially."

"Of course. There's around a million and a half people in the fourteen-county statistical area surrounding Nashville. The Titans' stadium has been sold out since the first game. The Predators have struggled, but we're holding our own. In my opinion, adding a basketball team to the mix would be disastrous."

"So what can you do to prevent that from happening?"

Franklin folded his hands and looked down at them for a moment. "Frankly, that's out of my area of expertise."

The interview seemed to be going nowhere until Jill switched the conversation to a more chatty note. "How did you become such an avid hockey fan, Mr. Franklin?"

He turned his high-back leather executive chair to face her, displaying a smile for the first time. "I'd never seen a big league professional hockey game until I joined the Marines and was sent to Camp Pendleton, California. I got to watch a few L.A. Kings' games and was hooked. After I left the service, I studied accounting in Boston and became a Bruins fan."

"Are you originally from Nashville?" Jill asked.

"Yes. I grew up here, but that was in the sixties. The only ice hockey back then was the Dixie Flyers. The Municipal Auditorium ice was a small, cramped rink. I remember hearing that in the early days the team traveled to out-of-town games in a former school bus."

"Did you go to any of their games?" I asked.

"A few, but it was nothing like this. I played hockey as a kid, but that was on roller skates out in the street. We used to flatten a tin can to use as a puck. My dad ran a Rexall drugstore out Hillsboro Road."

Jill turned to me. "I think I patronized that drugstore. You remember I lived out that way."

Her dad, who died a few years after we married, was a highly successful life insurance agent. They lived in a fancy area that gave me a real shock the first time I visited her large fieldstone home. It looked like a mansion to me, the son of a St. Louis master brewer and an English teacher.

"I'm retired Air Force," I said. "How long were you in the Marines?"

"Three years. I was injured in Vietnam and got out when I came back. That newspaper story about Wechsel mentioned he was from Germany. Have you learned anything about him from over there?"

"His uncle is a former colleague of mine," I said. "We're committed to tracking down who's responsible for Arnold Wechsel's death. Our main effort, though, is to find out what's behind this so-called rumor, which doesn't sound like a rumor at all. We plan to look deeper into the NBA backers, starting with Louie Aregis. We have one good lead we hope will pay off."

I decided not to go into detail. Although the CPA was one of Protect Our Preds' major benefactors, Terry Tremont had said Bradley Smotherman was the official client responsible for our being hired. My law enforcement experience had taught me that people tended to exaggerate or misinterpret information frequently. Spreading around too much about a case could quickly complicate matters.

When we left a short time later, Jill took me to task over what I had said. She gave me a squinty eye and dropped her voice to a skeptical tone. "What's that good lead we're expecting to pay off, dear?"

"I'm inclined to go with a mother's intuition," I said. "I think the gambling angle involving Arnold Wechsel is worth digging into a lot more deeply."

At the moment, however, I had no idea where to turn to pursue that possibility.

12

NASHVILLE DRIVERS handle winter weather in one of two ways. They either dash madly like mail carriers facing a deadline to deliver despite rain or snow or heat or gloom of night, or they creep along as though the streets were glazed over. On the way back to the office, we navigated a perilous path between both types as a mixture of rain and sleet pelted the windshield. Our only mad dashing came when we parked a couple of rows out from the small family restaurant at the opposite end of the shopping center.

"So what are the sleuths eating today?" asked Tillie, our usual waitress, or female server as my PC friends would say. A yellow pencil appeared from the graying hair above her ear. Round spectacles joined it in a vertical position, as if she had eyes in the top of her head. I suspected she did.

"I'll have that nice fruit salad you've been pushing lately," Jill said. "I don't know where you're getting the fruit this time of year, but it seems really fresh."

"The boss has a secret source at the Farmer's Market. I think it's a Florida farmer." Tillie nodded her head at me. "What about the old guy?"

I gave her the eye rolling routine. "The old guy would like a nice, juicy steak, but he'll settle for a nice, fresh fruit salad."

"He's on his good behavior these days," Jill said, smiling.

As the waitress flounced off to the kitchen, I gave Jill a look. "Thanks for that vote of confidence."

"It's true. I don't believe you've gained a pound lately. Of course, you haven't lost one, either."

She kept me on a short leash, but her magical touch made our low-fat, low-calorie dishes tasty.

"Enough chit-chat, babe," I said, "you're still on the clock. What did you think of Gordon Franklin?"

"I have a hard time picturing that Mr. Milquetoast as a Marine."

"That limp could've been service-connected."

"He didn't say he was wounded. I'll bet he broke his leg when he tripped over his calculator."

"That's not being very charitable," I said, emphasizing it with a tsk tsk.

Tillie appeared with our coffee and poured. We didn't need to ask.

Jill took a tentative sip. "Good and hot."

"Always is here. Not like Brother Gordon. He's a cool customer. I got the impression he wasn't all that concerned about the possibility of skullduggery among the NBA people."

"Certainly not as much as Smotherman."

"Yeah. And he doesn't call his firm Puck and Stick Accountants, either."

"Booo." She twisted her nose.

"He livened up a bit when you got him talking about hockey, though."

"He'd have to be a big fan to put up the kind of money Terry was talking about."

"Right. But I have a feeling he's too busy crunching numbers to be of much help to us."

I put the subject on hold when our fresh fruit salads arrived.

BACK AT THE OFFICE, I got on the phone to Louisville while Jill updated the case file on Preds vs. NBA. I reached

Lieutenant Dobyns at the police department and explained that I was a retired OSI agent in Nashville who had prosecuted a drug dealer/courier from Louisville years ago. I told him about spotting Izzy Isabell in Nashville and asked if they had any information regarding him since his release from prison.

"I'm not aware of anything," he said, "but I can check it out. Do you have a contact in the Nashville Police Department?"

"Homicide Detective Phil Adamson," I said.

"I know Adamson. He did a seminar here a couple of years ago. I'm sort of constrained by policy from providing information except through another police agency."

"That's fine," I said. "Just call Phil if you come up with anything."

I checked in with Phil and told him about the conversation.

"You think this guy is still on your case after all these years?" he asked.

"It doesn't sound like he's changed. Worse, if anything."

"Okay. I'll let you know if I hear from Louisville."

With that out of the way, we sat around Jill's desk for a strategy session to prepare her for the interview with Aregis tomorrow morning.

"One thing we need to know is where the money's coming from to finance this deal," I said. "I'm sure we're talking about hundreds of millions of dollars. Is Aregis the investor, or is it his Coastal Capital Ventures?"

She skimmed a newspaper clipping from the file. "They haven't confirmed what team they're talking about, either, but this story speculates it could be the Sacramento Kings, Portland Trail Blazers or Minnesota Timberwolves."

"See if you can get him to name any people he's talked with."

"Wonder if he talked to Arnold Wechsel? Be nice if I could get his reaction to that name, wouldn't it?"

"True, but there's no way you could get into that. You might probe around a bit as to how he got interested in this deal. I didn't see anything in his background that would hint at a basketball connection."

Jill looked up from her notes. "Should I inquire into what caused him to move his business to Nashville?"

"Sure. It might be significant if his move was related to this NBA franchise. I'd doubt it, but it would be helpful to know."

We discussed several additional possibilities before winding up our session. Jill had one other bit of preparation for the interview. Being a whiz at computer graphics, she quickly dummied up a business card for Contributing Writer Jill Parsons (her maiden name) of *Sporting World Magazine*. She printed out a few to go in her billfold.

Afterward, we spent a little time tying up some loose ends on an insurance case we'd just finished, then took off early to get dressed for our annual Sunday School Class Christmas Party. We had been members of the class at Gethsemane United Methodist Church since moving to Hermitage a few years back. I was a reluctant participant at first, but my wife is a world-class persuader. We soon developed friendships that had served us well since. After dinner at a local restaurant, we would adjourn to the home of Sam and Wilma Gannon for a gift swap. Another Air Force retiree, Sam had gone from flying B-26 light bombers in Korea to handling the controls of giant C-17 Globemaster transport planes.

At the dinner I got stuck beside the class clown, a retired pharmacist in his seventies who fancied himself the reincarnation of Jack Benny. He did resemble Benny a little, with his round glasses and high forehead, and he had the requisite tight-lipped smile. But he didn't have the timing quite right. He made a dramatic pause before the punch line, then botched it.

Jill was luckier. She sat next to Wilma Gannon. They had become best friends since returning to Nashville, where both grew up though on opposite sides of town. The daughter of one-time missionaries to China, Wilma liked to say Jill was born with a silver spoon in her mouth while she arrived with wooden chopsticks.

The Gannons lived in a brick ranch not far from us. Though the neighborhood was like a chessboard in its uniformity, the architects had varied the building materials enough to keep the houses from resembling clones. The Gannons' spacious den glowed with candles large and small, abetted by winking strings of lights on a Christmas tree that tickled the ceiling. You could tell it was real by the fresh evergreen smell. Cookies and candy, crackers and dips vied for space on a long table anchored by a sparkling glass punch bowl. Ice cubes drifted in a concoction as red as blood spatters, though the others didn't likely view it in those terms. Folding chairs sat around the walls, where people drifted after loading up on the goodies.

Everyone had brought a wrapped gift to put under the tree. Sam strolled along with a basket of paper slips bearing numbers, and we each took one. Starting with the bearer of the number "1," we all trooped to the tree to choose a gift. Under the rules, you had to open the gift and show it around. The person with the next number could either take that gift or go to the tree. The third person to possess a particular gift kept it. Things got pretty raucous at times, such as when a prim little lady unwrapped a three-cup bra supplied by the class wag. He tried to look innocent, but everyone knew who to blame.

While the women cleaned up the gift wrap mess, I chatted with Sam, casually bringing up the NBA basketball deal. He grew up in a rural area south of Tulsa and met Wilma at the University of Oklahoma, where he played basketball. Though he'd never been a starter, he had the physique for it, being a few inches taller than my five-ten and a lot slimmer. I'd heard him talk about how Oklahoma City should have an NBA team.

"What do you think about this bunch wanting to bring a pro basketball team to Nashville?" I asked.

He leaned against a bookcase loaded with paperbacks. "I'd probably buy a season ticket if Wilma didn't object too vociferously."

"Know what you mean. We go to a Titans game occasionally, but I couldn't talk Jill into taking the season ticket route."

"Some of the guys I play basketball with over at the Y are really fired up about the possibility of a team here. They say the people putting the deal together are loaded with cash."

"This Aregis fellow seems to be the ringleader, from what I've seen."

"Right. They told me the deal has been simmering the past several months. Aregis came up from Florida because of his interest in it. They say he's a real smooth operator, has lots of connections."

"Any of your friends involved in it?"

"One of them works for Howard Hays at Dollar Deal Stores. He's apparently been involved in some of the negotiations."

"I wonder if they've talked to any teams about selling?"

"I don't think so," Sam said, grabbing a cookie from a dish as Wilma passed by. "At least it hasn't been mentioned."

"I'd never heard of the other fellow the paper said was an investor in the deal. Fred Ricketts is his name, I believe."

"I've heard the name, but nobody's said anything about him."

"The Predators folks don't seem too happy about it," I said.

"I suppose not," he said with a grin. "They would have some real competition for fans."

Talking to Jill on the way home, I passed along what I had learned from Sam. It made good background for her interview in the morning.

Our neighborhood appeared clear of lurking SUVs, but I patted the bulk of the Sig-Sauer pistol I carried now. It was lighter and easier to conceal than the Beretta I had used since my Air Force days.

I pulled into the driveway still unsettled about how to take that SUV sighting Sunday night. Was it related to Arnold Wechsel's murder and Terry Tremont's case? Was it simply a random thing that had no relation to us? When we arrived at the house and checked the answering machine, there was a call at 8:07 showing "Uknown Name, Unknown Number." They had listened to our message, then hung up.

Had somebody with an untraceable cell phone checked to see if we were at home? Could it have been Izzy Isabell?

I had a sudden thought and turned to Jill. "Is that box of old papers from my OSI days still in the walk-in closet?"

"Unfortunately. Every time I try to throw it out, you insist on keeping it like some stash of love letters from your deep, dark past."

"What do you know about such things? Have you been hanging onto letters from some old lover?"

She put her hands on her hips and gave a sensuous sway. "I might let you read them sometime. They're from a dashing young Air Force officer in Vietnam. Some of them get pretty steamy."

I popped her one on the bottom and headed for the closet. I hauled out the box that hadn't been opened in years. It contained copies of files from a few special cases I had kept for future reference. One of them was the investigation of First Lt. Izzy Isabell. I took it downstairs to the office and spread papers across the desk.

Isabell was assigned to a Strategic Air Command refueling unit at Seymour Johnson Air Force Base in Goldsboro, North Carolina. When high quality cocaine began showing up in the area, the local cops got concerned and asked for Air Force help. We picked up information suggesting the source could be on base. Working with a Goldsboro police officer, I got an informant to admit that the drug came from an aircrew member. We finally narrowed it down to a particular KC-135. We searched the aircraft thoroughly following a couple of missions that had landed in suspect areas, but found nothing.

Although I spent many years in the Air Force, I readily confess I do not like to fly. Even with my competent and trusted wife at the controls, I am not a happy passenger. My motto is feet and wheels should be kept firmly planted on the ground. However, this was a case where duty prevailed. I arranged for a mission to a location the DEA identified as rife with cocaine trafficking and flew along as a passenger. I posed as a Department of Defense civilian on a familiarization flight. The guys would've called it a joyride.

After a routine refueling operation, we spent a couple of hours on the ground before returning to base. The crew consisted of the pilot, co-pilot, navigator, and boom operator. I wasn't able to keep an eye on everybody while we were killing time, but I did the best I could. One thing I noticed, the navigator never let his briefcase out of his sight. He disappeared while I had coffee with the pilot. When I saw him again, he still wagged that briefcase at his side. It looked a bit heftier than before.

On the flight back, I identified myself to the pilot as an OSI agent and sent a message to my office to have a narcotics-sniffing dog handy when we landed. The dog found Izzy Isabell's briefcase fascinating. He sat alertly beside it on the ramp. His handler said it indicated he had found the scent of drugs. When I told Izzy to open it, he caught me with a sucker punch. I retaliated with a right cross that flattened him. That was back in the days when I was still scrappy. Our relationship went downhill from there. I found three bricks of cocaine in the leather case. That's three kilograms, or nearly seven pounds, which would have brought a tidy sum, even in the late eighties. Under interrogation, he admitted to bringing in dozens of bricks worth a small fortune. While he was locked up awaiting trial, Izzy talked to a cellmate about putting out a contract on me and another witness in the case. Fortunately, he trusted the wrong person.

When I returned the file to my storage box and stuck it back in the closet, I knew Arnold Wechsel's murder and Terry Tremont's sports melee were not the only problems I faced.

13

WE DROVE BOTH cars to the office the next morning. Jill soon bailed out for her interview with Louie Aregis. I felt she would be in no danger at Coastal Capital Ventures, but I made sure she had that nasty little snub-nosed .38 in her handbag. When I called Rod Jenson at Channel 4 to see when we could meet with him, surprisingly, he said, "Right now. Come on over."

I called Jill before she reached Coastal Capital Ventures. I told her I would talk to Jenson and we could compare notes when we made it back to the office.

The television station occupied a hilltop on the opposite side of town. Rush hour had almost ended, but I-40 was still no picnic. I arrived to find a saucy redhead at a reception desk in the lobby, an area with two large windows that looked down on the studio and its news set. Having visited TV stations before, I always marveled at how cramped the studios looked up close compared with how they appeared on a TV screen. It was a profusely lighted room stuffed with cameras, an anchor desk, a weather nook, and sets where news and sports reporters stood to introduce their stories.

"I know Rod's around here somewhere," the receptionist said. "Let me see if I can scare him up for you."

She punched a few numbers, spoke into the phone, and looked up with a smile. "He'll be right out."

Jenson appeared a few minutes later and ushered me into a conference room with a long table surrounded by comfortable chairs. About my height, at least ten years younger, he gave me a smile that rumpled his broad brow, well-tanned despite the season. He had the casual, breezy look of a man who enjoyed living on the edge.

"I didn't realize how long it would take you to get here," he said as we took our seats. "I have to do an interview shortly. I'm not usually here this time of day."

"I should have warned you I was on the other side of the county. I promise not to take much of your time."

"Tell me what you're looking for. From what you said on the phone, it sounds like you're talking about the effort to bring an NBA team to Nashville."

I gave a noncommittal shrug. "It's related to that, but I can't tell you anything about the client."

His laugh was a muffled rumble. "You sound like a coach declining to talk about a quarterback change. I'll accept that."

"What are some of the hurdles a group would face in bringing a professional sports team to town?"

"I'd say raising lots of cash would rank number one. In the current situation, they seem to have mastered that with two well-heeled local businessmen and this venture capital guy from Florida. You'd need to line up sponsors, too, corporations willing to shell out cash to help get things set up. The most important hurdle, of course, would be attracting fans and selling tickets. That would require a major publicity campaign."

"Do you think Nashville can support three teams, NFL, NHL and NBA?"

"In a word, no."

"Which one would lose out?"

"My newspaper colleagues are more inclined to speculate on that. I don't mind giving you my take on it, though. With annual sellouts and a long waiting list for season tickets, the Titans have a lock on their share. The Preds also have an established fan base, though hardly on the same scale. Basketball would have to build from scratch. Still, it could go either way."

"If a basketball team comes in, would they likely share the same arena with the Predators?"

"They'd have to. Nashville isn't about to build another indoor monster downtown. It would require a lot of coordination in scheduling."

"Is this a typical ownership situation for a major league sports franchise, a group of local businessmen?"

Jenson pulled a pen from his pocket that resembled a giant golf tee and tapped it on the desk. "Actually, it's one of two ownership patterns. The other is a single millionaire like Bud Adams. He started the Titans as the Houston Oilers back in 1959. For group ownership, it isn't necessarily local. Could be guys from anywhere. who have to have a passion for sports."

I had been taking notes but put my small pad back in my pocket. "This question is a bit different and doesn't involve basketball or hockey. I understand some gamblers bet on NASCAR races. Do you know how that works?"

"You have rather eclectic interests, Mr. McKenzie," he said, the big grin returning.

"The hazards of the profession," I said.

"Personally, I'm not a gambler. Except for the lottery now and then. That's really not a gamble. Just a contribution to education. I'm familiar with betting on auto racing, though. It involves bets on race winners, sometimes on qualifying, also driver matchups."

"What are driver matchups?"

"It's preferred by professional gamblers. With forty-three drivers in the field, it's a crap shoot to pick a winner. With matchups, you pick two drivers and bet on which will finish ahead of the other."

"That should improve your chances, I'd think."

"You can keep the same matchup through the season or change from time to time."

I saw him check his watch. "Thanks for the information," I said, getting up. "That should give me a good start. I won't keep you any longer."

We shook hands. "Glad to help," he said. "Just give me a call if you need anything else."

JILL AND I MADE IT back to the office at about the same time. After shedding our coats and getting cappuccino cups in hand, which felt good to my freezing paws, we gathered at her desk. I started with a recounting of my Rod Jenson interview. After that, I pressed Jill for some tasty morsels.

"What's Louie Aregis like?"

"He's shorter than I expected," she said, "but very handsome. Still has his Florida tan. From the way he treated me, I'd say he's quite the ladies' man."

"Sounds provocative. Should I be worried?"

She shifted those big brown eyes. "He doesn't have that cute grin of yours."

I almost believed her. "What else does Mr. Aregis have?"

"Judging by the photos around his office and plaques on the wall, it appears that he has a love for outdoor sports, golf and tennis in particular. He also had an award from a shooting competition with a replica of a pistol mounted on it."

"That's interesting. Was he short enough that he could have fired an upward trajectory into Arnold Wechsel's head?"

Her face lit up with a sudden realization. "I hadn't thought of that, but you're right. It certainly could have happened that way."

"Unfortunately, we're a long way from having any proof that Aregis might be guilty of murder."

She gave a slight tilt to her head, which I took to mean she was reserving judgment.

"Where did he get his interest in pro basketball?" I asked.

"He claimed he was a big basketball fan in college but never had much opportunity for exposure at the professional level. Then the Charlotte Hornets moved to New Orleans, and he got excited, started thinking how nice it would be to own a basketball team."

I shifted my eyes away from the distraction of Jill's bouncing screensaver. "Did he say how he got involved in the Nashville deal?"

"He implied that it came about when some local businessmen approached him because of his experience with venture capital."

"Not exactly the way Sam's friends at the Y put it."

"No, it isn't. But that's his story."

"He must think a team can be successful here."

"He told me that surveys have shown a great deal of interest in basketball around Nashville."

"He doesn't think the fan base is saturated by the Titans and the Preds?"

"He says the Preds will probably struggle, but he thinks three teams can survive here."

"That's not Rod Jenson's take on it." I took a sip on the cappuccino, found it cool enough to drink, then asked, "How did you approach him on the question of why he came to Nashville?"

"I just asked if his move here was related to the NBA business. He claimed it resulted from several factors. Number one, this is a growing, progressive city. Number two, he has some good clients here and there's lots of wealth in the area. And number three—you'll love this one—his wife is a big country music fan."

I shook my head. "So he denied the basketball deal was responsible for his moving here."

"Not in those exact words. Aregis should be a politician. Instead of answering a question directly, he shifts the focus to what he wants to get across. I'd say the NBA was a major influence, but he doesn't want to admit it."

"Did you ask who some of his local clients are?"

That brought a grin. "He wasn't at liberty to discuss that. I mentioned all the colleges and universities in Nashville and asked if any were limited partners in his venture capital funds."

"And he said...?"

"He couldn't say."

"So what did he want to talk about?"

"Well, he didn't mind painting a glowing picture of what a great job Coastal Capital Ventures is doing. They've been endorsed by all sorts of people, like TV and movie stars. You name it."

"How did he size up the deal for a basketball franchise?"

"He says they've had discussions with some teams that might be possible candidates for relocation to Nashville. He wouldn't give a figure on how much money they're willing to spend but said they have enough to buy any team they're interested in."

"Will Coastal Capital be an investor?"

"Now you're asking specifics. Mr. Aregis doesn't like to get specific about anything. Remember how I boned up on those three teams and their players? He wasn't interested in talking about any of them. I got to wondering if he even knew who they were. One point he did make was that they had contacted the NBA commissioner's office to show they were a legitimate owner group."

When the phone rang, Jill looked at the caller ID and said, "Germany."

I answered it.

"Greg, this is Jeff," said my one-time OSI colleague. "We've come up with a bit of a puzzle."

"How so?" I asked.

"Arnold's body arrived today, along with his personal effects. They included something we can't figure."

"What's that?"

"A Saint Christopher's medal. It appears to be solid silver. Old Chris is the patron saint of Baden, which is part of the state of Baden-Wurttemberg, just to the southeast of here. The medal was attached to a silver chain. It was packed in a box along with his billfold and a few other things they apparently found in his pockets."

"So what's the problem?"

"For one thing, the Wechsels aren't Catholic. For another, it has a name engraved in small letters on the back—'N. Columbo.'"

"I presume the family has no knowledge of an N. Columbo?"

"Not a clue. I shot a picture of it. I'll email you a copy."

Could it have any significance to the mystery surrounding Arnold Wechsel's death? We were in the process of assembling a large jigsaw puzzle designed to answer the question of what had happened to him. I didn't intend to leave any pieces on the table.

14

I REPEATED JEFF Price's story for Jill, then called Detective Adamson and left a message on his voice mail.

"I presume you plan to write off your gift to Fingers O'Malley," Jill said.

I did my bull snort impression. "Let's head out to Dickerson Pike and see if we can find Fingers. It's time we had a few choice words with Mr. O'Malley."

We took Briley Parkway past Opry Mills Mall and the massive Opryland Resort and Convention Center complex. The Mall appeared loaded with Christmas shoppers, but this season was a lull time for conventions at the hotel. Just as well, the way the weather had been lately. Yesterday's rain and sleet mixture had passed on, leaving folds of heavy, dark clouds chased by a cold, gusty wind. We made a short jog on I-65 to the Trinity Lane exit and found the A&R Café a short way down Dickerson Pike. It occupied a small building sandwiched between a dry cleaner and a hardware store. Tommy Carroll turned out to be the owner, the chef, and the headwaiter.

"Have you seen Fingers O'Malley this morning?" I asked.

A short, squat man with eyes as big as silver dollars, he wiped chunky hands on his white apron. "You must be Mr. McKenzie."

"That's right. I need to talk to Mr. Fingers."

"He was in here a little while ago. He's got money. Even paid for his coffee."

I gave him a pained smile. "Some of my money."

"I figured you must have beefed up his bank account. Did you not get your money's worth?"

"The information he gave me was hardly accurate."

"Sorry. He means well, but he's not the sharpest blade on your pocketknife. I'm pretty sure he headed up the street. You'll probably find him at the grocery store on the next corner."

I thanked him, and we drove to the market. Looking around inside, we spotted him leaning against the deli counter, munching on a handful of crackers. He grinned at us as we walked up. His nose looked redder than his eyes today.

"Bring my other fifty?"

"Hardly," I said. "I'd like to get back the fifty I gave you, but it's probably been spent already."

"How come you want it back?"

"That license number you gave us was for a yellow Volkswagen Beetle, not a black SUV."

His frown carried a puzzled look. "Cain't be. I writ what I seen."

I looked at those cloudy eyes and diagnosed the problem. Pointing at a poster across the store, I asked, "What does that sign say?"

He squinted at it. "Somethin' 'bout grapes. I ain't too good at readin'."

"What are the numbers in the price?"

"Uh...looks like two...uh, three...five."

The grapes were priced at $2.86. "Have you ever had your eyes checked for glasses?" I asked.

"How you 'spect me to afford them fancy things?"

"Some civic organizations sponsor free eye clinics now and then. I'd advise you to check it out next time you hear of one. Keep the fifty bucks. That's our charitable contribution for the week."

IT WAS AFTER LUNCH when Phil Adamson returned my call.

"I just heard from the Louisville PD," he said. "Izzy Isabell showed up in his old neighborhood last weekend. His parents still live there. They reported he was high on drugs and abusive. They told him they didn't have room for him to live there, that he'd have to find some place else. He said he might go to Nashville, he had a friend here."

"Did they mention what he was driving?" I asked.

"Said he had a blue Ford truck."

"That's what I saw him in. Didn't get a look at the license plate. I wonder if he's tapped into the drug money he stashed away before I caught him?"

"You think the money might be here?"

"I have no idea."

"Louisville is sending me a recent photo," Phil said. "Want me to pass it around, see if anybody might spot him?"

"It would be good to know where he is in case anything happens. And by the way, I had another call from Germany today. What can you tell me about Arnold Wechsel's Saint Christopher medal?"

"He was wearing it on a chain around his neck when he was shot."

"I figured it was either that or in his pocket. Did you notice the engraved name on the back?".

"Columbo. Did his folks identify it as somebody in Germany? I haven't found anybody with that name around Nashville."

I studied the photo of the medal on my desk, printed out from Jeff Price's email. "The Wechsels had never heard of N. Columbo either."

"It may not mean anything, but I'll keep looking."

I intended to, also. "Have you turned up anything new on the homicide?" I asked.

"I measure progress with this investigation in millimeters. We checked his phone records for the past few days. Nothing but calls to work and this Ullery guy. He didn't have a cell phone on him. Neither his check register nor his credit card receipts showed any payments to cell phone companies. Matter of fact, he apparently used his credit card infrequently. What about you? Making any progress with the hoopsters?"

"If talk is progress. We're doing plenty of that. But nobody's said anything that puts a sign on the roadmap showing any destinations."

"Tell me about it."

When I got off the phone, I found Jill sitting at her desk with that Cheshire cat grin.

"Okay," I said. "Get that mouse from between your teeth."

"I've been on the computer," she said with a smug look. "There's no Columbo in the phone book, but I found one through Peopledatascan dot com. They give more details than anybody. I think they must have a back door to the credit bureau. She's Nicole Columbo, a twenty-three-year-old from Memphis who works at an Italian restaurant in Green Hills."

"N. Columbo. It has to be her. Looks like our boy had a girlfriend after all."

"She's probably a hostess or a waitress. I'll see if she's working tonight. We can go eat Italian and I won't have to fix anything for supper."

I ran my tongue around my lips. "I could use a little manicotti, maybe some cannelloni."

She lifted a sculpted brow. "And I'll need to keep an eye on your portion control."

"That's not all we need to keep an eye on," I said. "Phil said the Louisville cops confirmed my sighting. Izzy Isabell returned home last weekend and left for Nashville in a blue pickup."

Her eyes flashed in alarm. "Coming after you?"

"I wish I knew. He told his parents he had a friend in Nashville."

With a few new developments in hand, I called Terry Tremont to update him on what we'd learned about Arnold Wechsel and Louie Aregis.

"So Aregis is apparently lying about how he got into this deal," Terry said, a note of disgust in his voice. "Sounds like he may be the faulty link in this chain."

"Could be, but we haven't found a way to exploit it yet. We've come up with a new angle that we plan to check out, though."

I summarized the story of Nicole Columbo and the Saint Christopher's medal. Having watched Terry at work in his office, I knew he would be taking notes on everything I had to say. That was one reason for his success in court. He missed nothing.

"My wife's Italian," he said. "I'm familiar with the Italian community around Nashville. I've never heard of any Columbos."

"She's from Memphis. I'd like to know how she met Wechsel and what their relationship was. He could have been a customer at the restaurant. We plan to go by there tonight and check her out."

"I'll be interested in what you find. Getting back to the NBA folks, what have you learned about Fred Ricketts? Everybody knows the Howard Hays story, but Ricketts seems a bit of a question mark."

"I read an interesting magazine article about how he put P and S Software on the map. I haven't learned much about him personally, though."

"I may have the answer," Terry said. "I have a client I who just learned worked with Ricketts when he was a big shot at the hospital chain a few years ago. Name's Ken Vickers. He runs a company that deals with hospital supplies. Why don't you give Ken a call. Tell him I'd like him to help you with some background on Ricketts. See what he has to say."

Vickers was in a meeting and wouldn't be out for another hour. I left word that I needed to talk to him, then explained what was going on to Jill.

"Since you have an hour to kill," she said, "you can make a run to the office supply store and get a carton of copy paper. All these data searches are about to deplete our supply."

I drove to a nearby shopping center and parked in front of the store. As I was about to get out, I glanced at the rearview mirror and saw a large black SUV moving slowly behind me. I popped the door open and jumped out, but I wasn't fast enough. I caught a glimpse of the car as it turned between two rows of vehicles and headed out of the lot.

Damn! I slammed the Jeep's door and fumed. If it was the one we had seen Sunday night, I had just missed a chance for a positive ID.

Then I leaned back and took a deep, cold, sobering breath. It could have been anybody. Some people actually drove slowly through parking lots to keep from hitting someone. Was I getting uptight over an incident that, for all we knew, had nothing to do with us? I didn't believe that. Something was going on and I wanted to know what.

When I came out of the store and reached to open the car door, my eyes nearly bugged out at what I saw. A long, jagged scratch ran from just under the side mirror, across both doors, back to the quarter panel. I hadn't been keyed. It looked more like I'd been awled. I shoved the box into the back seat, then stood there and fumed. That was when I spotted the note under the wiper. It read:

"The guy who did it got into a blue pickup. I couldn't get his license number."

15

"THAT BASTARD Isabell scratched hell out of my Jeep," I announced in a loud voice as I stormed into the office.

Jill looked at me with a frown that could have been a cross between indignation at my outburst and despair at my message. I showed her the note and told her what happened, then carried the large box of paper over to the counter. After taking out a ream and refilling the drawer of our combination printer-copier- scanner- fax machine, I noticed the sheet in the output tray.

"When did this come in?" I asked. I took the sheet and tossed it onto Jill's desk.

"Just now. I hadn't had time to check it out." She stared at the photo. "It's Isabell, isn't it?"

He looked about as I remembered him. Angular face, short hair, intense eyes, but a bit rougher and more weathered.

"That's the..." I let it drop as her frown intensified.

"Fortunately, he directed his mischief at your Jeep instead of yourself," she said.

I sat at my desk and thought of wicked things I might do if we were to meet. Before I got too far, the phone rang. Ken Vickers.

I told him about Terry Tremont's suggestion.

"I haven't been involved with Ricketts since he left to form his own business," Vickers said, "but I still see him once in a while. He's one of those driven guys. You know, not happy unless he's involved in some sort of action. He took off like a rocket when he started that company. Now he's about to make a fortune off of it."

"Which he's prepared to spend on a basketball franchise," I said. "Has he always been a big sports fan?"

"He's part owner of an Indy race car and always went up to The 500 to see his car run. I'd say this is just another way to get in on the action."

I thought of all we'd learned about Arnold Wechsel. "Is Ricketts a gambling man?"

"He likes to beat the odds. He's not afraid to take a chance if he thinks it'll pay off."

"Are you referring to business decisions or making bets?"

"As for bets, he might make a friendly wager, but probably only if he thought it was a sure thing."

"I read where he's in his thirties, a fairly young guy. How did he get such a good job with the hospital outfit at such an early age?"

Vickers spoke with the formidable voice of a big man. I could picture a hulking body hovering over his desk. He had a ready answer for every question.

"Fred was a computer whiz kid out of college," he said. "One of the top people in the company latched onto him and pushed him up in the ranks."

"Did he leave the hospital business to start his software company?"

Vickers gave a little chuckle. "In a manner of speaking. What happened was he had the idea for this new venture and began trying to put it together while still working under his mentor at the company. His boss got wind of it and was not the least bit pleased. He suggested it was time for Fred to devote full-time to the new business."

"In other words, he was invited to leave."

"That's as good a way of putting it as any. I worked in the office across from his, and I can tell you he was furious as a scalded hornet. Turned out it was the best thing for him, but he had a lot of deleted expletives for his boss."

Fred Ricketts sounded like a man I needed to know more about. "I'd like to meet him, preferably in a relaxed, informal atmosphere. Do you know of any place he frequents?"

He paused for a moment. "Are you familiar with Contacts Nashville?"

"Nope."

"It's a group that sponsors a couple of get-togethers each month to bring business and professional people together for networking. I don't go to all of them, but Fred has been there every time I've attended."

"Is it like a cocktail party, or what?"

"They mix and mingle and have lunch. They're meeting now at the Bull and Boar Steakhouse in Brentwood. It's normally only open for dinner, so they have the whole place to themselves."

Ricketts' company was located in Brentwood, an upscale town on the edge of Williamson County just south of Nashville. Williamson had one of the highest per capita incomes of any county in the U.S.

"When do they meet?" I asked.

"The second and fourth Wednesdays. That would make it tomorrow. I don't know about Christmas week, though. I can check to make sure. The sessions are open to anyone, so all you have to do is show up."

He called back a few minutes later to confirm that Contacts Nashville would meet tomorrow at 11:30 a.m. I told Jill we had a lunch date for in the morning.

WE ARRIVED EARLY at the Villa d'Este Restaurant, hoping

to catch Nicole Columbo before things got too busy. I came through the foyer, blowing warmth into my freezing hands, and passed a gaily-decorated tree filled with winking colored lights. We were met by a young woman slightly taller than me, with long black hair and a pretty face. She had high cheekbones accented by a wide smile.

"Two for dinner?" she asked.

I answered with a confirming nod. She looked about the right age for the girl we'd come to see. She pulled two menus from a stack and led us into the dining area, where Dean Martin's voice trilled *That's Amore* for the benefit of three tables of diners. It was a typical mid-range restaurant, lush greenery, subdued lighting, almost too dim to see the prices.

As she laid the menus on the table, I smiled and asked, "Are you by chance Nicole Columbo?"

Her large, dark eyes popped open wide. "Do I know you?"

"We've never met, but I'm the one who found Arnold Wechsel at the auto repair shop three nights ago."

Her face paled. She looked ready to cry. I felt sorry for her and wished I had phrased my introduction with a bit more subtlety.

Jill gently took her hand. "We're very sorry about what happened, dear. I hope you'll forgive us for upsetting you."

Nicole Columbo looked from Jill to me. "How did you...know...about me?"

"We found out quite by accident," I said. "Arnold's aunt is married to a friend of mine. He told me there was a Saint Christopher's medal among the things they sent back to Germany. It had your name engraved on the back."

Nicole pulled a tissue from the pocket of her slacks and dabbed at her eyes. "But it only said 'N. Columbo.'"

"Yes, dear," Jill said, "but we're private investigators. It's our business to find out such things."

She bit at her lower lip, obviously struggling to maintain her composure, and glanced at me. "I remember now. The private investigator thing. It was in the newspaper story."

"Arnold called and asked me to meet him there," I said. "We'd like to talk to you about it."

She swung her head toward the front of the restaurant, where a few customers had come in. "I'm sorry...I have to go."

She hurried away.

Jill looked across at me as we took our seats. "Did you notice the change in her expression when you said we'd like to talk to her about what happened?"

"It was fear. Why would she be afraid to talk to us?"

"We need to find out," Jill said.

When the waitress came, we ordered the three-cheese manicotti and a bottle of Zinfandel. I had no trouble devouring my portion while discussing what we knew about Nicole Columbo, which was not enough to explain her reaction. Jill had a generous helping on her plate when the waitress stopped by to see if we had finished.

"Would you like a take-out box?" she asked.

"No thanks," Jill said. "I have enough leftovers at home already. It was delicious, though."

Few additional customers had come in while we were eating. I figured Tuesday must be a slow night. I'm sure the deep freeze outside didn't help. It was fortunate for us, though, since it meant less likelihood of distraction when we stopped to corner Nicole on our way out.

We took our time, hoping the longer she had to think about it, the more likely she would be to answer our questions. We lingered over the Zinfandel, then ordered coffee and tiramisu for dessert. To keep Jill from objecting, I suggested we share a serving of the tasty concoction. It brought me high marks. According to Jill, it appeared to be made from the original

Italian recipe, which called for a round shape containing savoirdi biscuits, or lady fingers, soaked in expresso and layered with a mixture of mascarpone cheese, eggs, sugar and honey. Cocoa powder was sprinkled on top.

After deciding we had dallied long enough, I signed the credit card receipt. We donned our winter gear and headed for the entrance. As we approached, I noticed a sticky note on the edge of the stand where the hostess stood. It bore the name "Nikki."

"I'm so sorry we upset you," Jill said in a motherly tone. "Believe me it was not our intention."

Nikki Columbo gave her a meek smile. "It's all right. I shouldn't have been so sensitive. I'm starting to get over it, but the past few days have been unbelievable."

"The police don't know about you, and we'd like to keep it that way," I said. "Keep you from becoming involved in the investigation."

Her eyes turned wary. "I'd appreciate that."

"At the same time," Jill said, "it's our duty to help them find who did this terrible thing to Arnold. You can help by letting us sit down and talk to you. There may be some things you don't realize you know that could help us track down the person responsible."

Nikki listened in silence.

"When would be a good time to call you tomorrow?" Jill asked.

Nikki breathed heavily and looked down with unseeing eyes at the seating chart on the slanted stand in front of her.

Jill waited.

Nikki finally looked up and said, "I don't know. Let me think about it."

I handed her a business card as a draft of cold air hit our backs and two couples walked in.

"I'll call you," Nikki said, glancing at the card, then turned toward the new customers.

 **16**

ALTHOUGH WE HAD dined leisurely, we arrived home at a decent hour. Jill returned a call from Wilma Gannon and curled up in her recliner. I had learned early on that any chat with Wilma would be an extended one. I headed upstairs to the bedroom and returned my Sig to its accustomed place in the bedside table drawer. After retreating to the kitchen, I pulled down a container labeled "Spiced Tea" that had the appearance of a jar filled with orange sand. It looked like a good nightcap for a cold winter evening since I wasn't in a mood for more wine, and I didn't like to mix Scotch and Zinfandel.

I heated water, shoveled orange sand into a cup, stirred it a bit, and moved to the table. As I sipped it slowly, I thought about our confrontation with Nikki Columbo. I had chosen to let Jill do the talking since her motherly manner went over well with the younger set. You'd never know she had no children of her own. Nevertheless, it wasn't an easy sell. Would Nikki call us back? That earlier look of fear still bugged me. Who or what was she afraid of? Jill had said we would try to shield her from the police, and that would mean holding back from Phil Adamson. Hardly something new. What we needed was to bore in on her relationship with Arnold Wechsel. I decided to pursue her background a lot deeper and see if we could turn up something that would provide a hint about the problem she was bent on hiding.

When I got down to the dregs, I rinsed my cup and put it in the dishwasher, then headed for the living room. Jill still had the phone anchored to her ear. I took up my position beside her, listening to an occasionally muttered "I know what you mean" or "did she really say that?" Punching on the TV remote, I muted the sound and watched some fictional CSI guys and gals pull off their miraculous feats. Like most professional law enforcement types, I marveled at the fantastic advancements of forensic science but watched in dismay at the way they were portrayed on TV.

Jill finally turned to me and held out the phone. "Sam wants to talk to you."

I gave him a cheery greeting. "How are things in the wild blue yonder?"

"Ha, the only wild blue I've seen lately was the jeans hanging halfway down some young hooligan's butt at the drugstore. What's up with you?"

"From the sounds in my stomach, I'd guess I'm digesting all that Italian food I ate at the Villa d'Este Restaurant."

"Been stepping out with your lady, huh? Good for you. What I wanted to ask about, I got the idea last night that you're more than a little interested in this NBA proposal. True?"

Sam knew me too well. I was afraid something like that might happen. "True, but it isn't something I can talk about. If you hear anything else, though, I'd appreciate your passing it along."

"I was playing 'horse' with my friend from the Dollar Deal Stores today—he let's me beat him now and then—and he started talking about that situation again."

"What's going on now?"

"Seems the commissioner's office contacted them. Wanted more background on everybody who'll have any ownership interest in the team."

"They want to be sure there's nothing unsavory about any of them."

"That's what he said. When he mentioned something about Aregis, I asked how the new guy from Florida got into the picture. According to him, Aregis got wind of their efforts somehow and contacted them about getting in on the action."

"Interesting. I'm sure they looked into his background before inviting him in."

"He said Mr. Ricketts had known Aregis before."

I thought about that a moment. "I wonder if Ricketts was an investor in Coastal Capital Ventures?"

"He didn't say. Like me to see what else I can get from him?"

I didn't want to risk getting too inquisitive. "Better to just listen to what he has to say. Don't get too obvious about it."

When I told Jill what the dollar store fellow had said, she gave a "hmph" of disgust. "So much for Louie Aregis' believability."

"I wonder what else he lied about?"

"Couldn't have been much, since he didn't tell me a lot."

"It sounds like he muscled his way into this group, doesn't it?"

"He's a manipulator and a world class bamboozler."

I had run into his kind before. They were the guys who sold refrigerators in the Arctic Circle and heaters to the natives in Equatorial Africa. I was a little surprised that sophisticated businessmen would hook up with such a character, but Fred Ricketts had apparently had some sort of relationship with him in the past. No doubt they considered his status as a venture capitalist a plus in negotiating a deal.

A beep-beep sounded from the alarm system. It was similar to the signal for an outside door opening, except for the tone. This one meant the exterior floodlights had been tripped. I went to the front door and looked out. It normally indicated a car was approaching on the driveway. I saw nothing.

"Who is it?" Jill asked.

"Nobody. That's odd."

"Could it have been a dog?"

"A dog won't do it. It takes at least a man-sized object."

"Maybe it was a deer."

"When have we seen a deer around here, Jill? I'm going out and take a look around the place."

She jumped up and grasped my arm. "Be careful, Greg. Take your weapon."

I grabbed my Beretta from the downstairs office, stuck it in my belt in back, pulled on my jacket, and hurried outside. Muffled traffic noises from adjacent streets and the solitary bark of a neighbor's dog broke the stillness. A freezing breeze out of the north bore the smell of woodsmoke as it nipped at my nose. I made a quick circle of the house, letting my gaze sweep the perimeter of the property. We were surrounded by trees, except for the driveway opening and a gap that allowed us a glimpse of the Rogers' house next door. Everything appeared in order, with neither man nor beast in sight. The second time around, I walked slowly, checking every spot where somebody or something might choose to hide. In an area near the garage, I saw what looked like a footprint. When I stooped beside it, though, I realized it was a slight depression where water had frozen.

Back inside, I shed my jacket and tossed it onto a chair.

"What did you find?" Jill asked.

"A lot of fog from breathing out in that cold air. But nothing that would have triggered the floods. Whatever or whoever it was must have been scared off when the lights flashed on."

"Do you think it was some*body*? Like that ex-lieutenant who defaced your car?"

"I wish I knew, but I don't. To quote one of my old OSI instructors, 'If you have no clue, admit it.'"

"When you add in that phone call last night and the SUV the night before, I'm not too happy about it."

I eased the clip from the Beretta, recalling the black SUV I'd seen this afternoon. "I forgot to tell you after that episode with the scratch, but I saw an SUV cruise by slowly just as I parked at the office supply store. It looked like the one from Sunday night, but it sped away before I could get a good look. I'm not happy at all about the way things are going. I don't intend to lose sleep over it, though."

I hoped I didn't lose anything else.

17

FLURRYING SNOW swirled about the next morning on our way to the office. The forecasters predicted no accumulation. Though the stores weren't open yet, it was looking a lot like Christmas, now only three days off. A woman sauntered away from her car toting a large shopping bag with colorful packages peeping out the top. Probably getting ready for a party at the medical clinic down the way. It reminded me that I hadn't bought anything for Jill. Not surprising, since I'm a Christmas Eve shopper.

Inside the office, a call from Terry Tremont awaited us.

He got right to the point. "Did that Columbo business bear any fruit?"

I told him about our conversation at the restaurant. I also related the information Sam had picked up from his basketball-playing friend at the YMCA.

"We've talked to a lot of people, and I'm convinced there's a scandal out there somewhere," I said. "We haven't been able to put a face on it, though Aregis is looking more like a possible candidate."

Terry replied in an edgy voice. "I hope you can give me some answers soon, Greg. From what that Dollar Deal fellow told your friend, it sounds like they may be a lot further along than we thought. I'll have to pass this on to the Preds folks. Gordon Franklin told me yesterday that you all had been by to see him. You still plan to talk to Mack Nolan?"

"When we can pin him down. Franklin wasn't much help. Said he left all the details up to Brad Smotherman and Nolan."

"Probably true," Terry said. "I met with the three of them originally, but Brad is the key man. Franklin is highly regarded in the accounting field, and he's obviously an avid hockey fan. He doesn't seem too interested in getting involved with the nitty-gritty of this campaign, though. He wanted to know what I thought of your investigation."

"I hope you weren't too hard on us," I said.

"I relayed some of the information you gave me yesterday and assured him you were working hard on the case. I expected you to have something definitive soon."

"That's certainly our intent."

When I put the phone down, Jill brought my cappuccino with a questioning frown. "We haven't been fired yet?"

"No, but we'd better start getting some results. Maybe a check into Nikki Columbo's background would yield something." I took a sip from my insulated travel mug and grimaced. "Wow, that's hot. I think I'll let it cool a bit while I go get some extra batteries for our spy gear."

"Take your time," Jill said. "Those cups hold heat like the cone of a volcano."

Flurries of snow twisted in the swirling gusts, peppering my face with needle pricks as I trudged along the row of shops, tightening my jacket collar. The battery store was next to the café on the opposite end from our office. About halfway down, a pickup truck caught my eye. A light blue Ford F-150.

I slowed my pace and casually looked around the area. The vehicle was empty. I saw no one else along the sidewalk.

The truck was parked in front of a store that sold women's handbags. I walked in and looked around.

"Can I show you something?" asked a small woman with graying hair and a friendly smile.

"I was looking for someone," I said.

"Unfortunately, you're my first customer today. Or almost customer."

"Sorry," I said, returning her smile, "but I'm not in the market for a bag. Is that your truck out front?"

"Oh, no. I drive a small car. The truck was there when I came in."

I walked out across the parking lot where I could see the license plate. It was a Tennessee plate, not Kentucky. Maybe it meant nothing, but as I turned toward the battery store, I wrote the number in my ever-handy note pad.

Back at the office, my cappuccino tasted great after coming in from the cold. I had just settled back into my chair when the phone rang and the caller ID showed R.T. Investigations with an 850 area code, meaning Pensacola, Florida.

"Hi, Red, you must have found an office," I said.

"I'm in business. Already have a couple of referrals."

"Great. Are you making any progress on Louie Aregis?"

"I've run into a few smoldering guns but no smoke. I intended to call you sooner, but I got tied up getting moved in."

"What sort of smoldering guns?"

"The Better Business Bureau has some complaints. They appear to be mostly from people who didn't make as much money off their investments as they thought they should've."

"Sore losers." I sipped on the cappuccino as Red replied.

"Mostly, but there was one who says Aregis cheated him out of a big chunk of change. I haven't been able to get in touch with him yet. I also found a recent employee who wasn't very complimentary. He says his former boss is a megalomaniac who thinks he's God's gift to the financial world. Aregis will exaggerate his importance at the drop of a celebrity."

"That's the impression Jill got when she interviewed him yesterday."

"She did? Good move. I trust he didn't know she was a detective?"

"Hardly. She posed as a writer for a sports magazine. Our case involves a plan to bring an NBA team to Nashville."

"Sounds like you've brought her up to speed on social engineering," he said with a chuckle.

That was a term used mostly by skip tracers to cover methods of getting information out of subjects by pretending to be someone else. "I think it helped that she did a little acting in school," I said.

"This ex-employee told me about the basketball deal. Said it was why Aregis left Pensacola. The guy wasn't invited to go with him. Claims he wouldn't have gone if he had been. He said Coastal Capital had lost some big clients recently and wasn't doing as well as Aregis would have you believe. He doubted his old boss had the cash to put up a big chunk for the NBA franchise."

"Then where would he get the money?"

"One of his current clients, probably."

"Aregis told Jill that he had some Nashville clients, but he wouldn't give any names. Do you think your guy would have any information on clients from up here?"

"I'll ask him. It may take a couple of days, though. He was going to Tallahassee for a meeting of some state agency."

"Okay. Let me know if you get any names. Our folks are getting antsy. Anything else we should know?"

"He said dealing with Aregis could be risky business. While he's normally all smiles, glad-handing everybody he meets, he hides a nasty temper that can explode if he's crossed. He's the get even type."

"Thanks, Red. We'll keep that in mind."

Could Arnold Wechsel have learned something about Louie Aregis that would have prompted the venture capitalist to commit murder? Was it the information Arnold intended to pass along that would blow my mind? We had heard nothing to indicate the young man even knew Aregis. Clearly, we had a lot more digging to do.

I found Jill at her computer scampering about the web. I looked over her shoulder and saw the name "Columbo."

"What have we here, babe?"

"I'm onto Miss Nikki's trail," she said. "I should have something shortly. What did Red have to report?"

I told her about the former Coastal Capital employee's comments.

"Sounds like I had Aregis figured out pretty well, huh?"

"You did good. Now if Red can identify some of Aregis's Nashville clients, we should have some decent leads to check out."

She typed in a new search term and looked around. "Are you thinking one of them could be the black sheep in this deal?"

"It's a possibility."

I went back to my desk and a few minutes later Jill dropped a sheet of paper in front of me.

"Nicole graduated from Rhodes College in Memphis. It's a small Presbyterian school, used to be called Southwestern. Her parents are Vincent and Belinda Columbo. He works at the FedEx headquarters in Memphis. Haven't found anything yet on mom."

"Why would a girl who graduated from college in Memphis come to Nashville to work at a restaurant?" I asked.

"We need to ask about that, if she agrees to talk to us."

"If she doesn't volunteer to talk," I said, "Mother McKenzie may have to put on a full court press."

Jill went back to her computer, and I put through a call to

Jeff Price at Ramstein Air Base. He had just come from interrogating a kid caught with a stash of cocaine.

"You'd think they'd know better," he said. "The Germans are a little lax about marijuana, but they won't tolerate coke."

"Some things don't change, Jeff. I called to let you know what we've come up with on that Saint Christopher's medal. We tracked down a girl named Nikki Columbo who's admitted to being the N. Columbo engraved on the back."

I told him about our encounter at the restaurant.

"Arnold's mother got a letter from him today that was mailed the day he died," Jeff said. "He told her he'd met a girl recently that he had really fallen for. He gave the name Nikki. But he added that a problem had cropped up he hoped wouldn't ruin things for them."

"Did he elaborate on the problem?"

"That was all he said."

"It may be why Nikki was reluctant to talk to us."

"Think she'll open up under pressure?"

"We may have to find out. PI's don't have the same leverage as OSI agents, though. We have to go about it with a little more finesse."

"I'll bet you can finesse the devil out of 'em, Colonel." The cackle he let out was so loud I had to pull the phone away from my ear.

Jill looked across at me when I finished the call. "That was some laugh. I could hear it all the way over here."

"Agent Price has a distinctive manner of demonstrating his glee, that's for sure. But he also provided some interesting news."

I relayed the message Arnold had written home.

"I also have a bit of news," she said. "Nikki Columbo's mother was Belinda Zicarelli. There are some Zicarellis in the Nashville phone book."

That gave me an idea. "Let's look into that restaurant in Green Hills. I'll see who owns it. You check on the real estate."

A couple of years ago, I had an all-too-brief tenure as an investigator for the District Attorney. It ended disastrously after my off-the-record comments about a muddle-headed Metro Murder Squad detective wound up on page one of the morning paper. I still had several good contacts around the courthouse, however, and it didn't take long to learn that the restaurant was owned by a corporation headquartered in Orlando.

I walked over to Jill's desk. "No local connection on the ownership."

She looked up. "Well, according to the county property records, the real estate is owned by Zicarelli Properties."

"There's our connection." I folded my arms with a satisfied grin. "Now we need to find out who is behind Zicarelli Properties and what relation they are to Nikki Columbo."

"That shouldn't be too difficult," Jill said.

I agreed. It was all part of that basic gumshoe work that I had alluded to in our talk with Brad Smotherman. But something else about this investigation was bugging me, something that lay hidden back in a dark corner of my mind. I couldn't spring it loose. That was one of the hazards of creeping up in the senior citizen ranks. Forgetting little details became easier and easier. I was confident something would trigger the memory. I just hoped it would happen sooner rather than later.

The phone rang, and Jill answered it.

"Hello, Phil," she said, then, after a moment, "Well, if you run across any bodies this morning, they should be well preserved. It's cold as the dickens out there."

As she listened, her expression grew more serious. "That's awful," she said. "Pity the poor mothers. They're always hit the hardest. Here, let me put Greg on. He can tell you what we've learned."

I took the phone. "What's awful?" I asked.

"Couple of kids shot over around Jefferson Street. Drug related, as usual. What was Jill talking about?"

"We found the girl who gave the Saint Christopher's medal to Wechsel."

"Who is she?"

"Nicole Columbo, a Memphis girl who works at a restaurant in Green Hills."

"Was she able to shed any light on my case?"

"We haven't been able to sit down with her yet. That's on our agenda for today."

I probably should have told him about the local connection, but I didn't want him scaring the hell out of Nikki, maybe driving her farther into her shell. I had high hopes that Jill could break down her defenses. Anyway, I knew he wasn't telling us all he knew, so why not reciprocate?

"If she knows anything that'll help my case, pass it along," Phil said.

"Will do. Have you come up with anything new?"

"We did one interview that put a damper on the gambling theory. Talked to some Superspeedway pit crew guys Wechsel had been cozying up to. Seems Arnold had mentioned something about gambling on the races. They warned him he could be barred from the pits if he so much as talked about gambling around there. According to the guys, he apparently took it to heart and never mentioned it again."

Maybe so, as far as gambling on the races, I thought. But Dick Ullery had talked about other kinds of gambling. What had Arnold Wechsel really been into?

After I checked the phone book and found no Zicarelli Properties, or anything close to it, I called a Realtor friend and asked about the company. She'd never heard of it, either. She said the account might be handled by a property rental firm. She'd ask around and let me know.

In her earlier data search, Jill had found Nikki Columbo's address at an apartment in the Green Hills area. When she looked for a telephone, she turned up a blank, either listed or unlisted. We guessed Nikki used only a cell phone, as we'd discovered many young people did these days. We tried a database where you could find cell phone numbers but came up empty-handed. She could have a new phone that wasn't in the database yet. If we didn't hear from her soon, we'd have to try catching her at home. We needed some answers.

$$\bullet\!\!\diagdown \quad \textbf{18}$$

WITH THE MERCURY climbing incrementally during the morning, a steady drizzle replaced the flurries. I held the umbrella for Jill but got a freezing shower before I could make it behind the wheel. We found the Bull and Boar Steakhouse in a building with a rustic look hardly reflective of pictures I'd seen of the plush interior. A couple of dozen cars already occupied the parking area. The first thing that caught my eye was a dark blue Cadillac Escalade sitting at the right of the restaurant's entrance. When I pointed it out to Jill, her lips parted and her face took on a look of total dismay.

"There's a black one in that row of cars over there," she said, pointing.

Complications. Even more disturbing, as I viewed the car in the daylight, I didn't feel all that certain this was the model we had seen on Chandler Road Sunday night. I was aware, however, that first impressions usually turned out the best.

A couple of animated young women at a table set up near the entrance got us registered, collected our money, and gave us badges with "Greg" and "Jill" in large letters. We wandered into the dining area, where a group of men and women clustered around tables of snacks, mostly of the chip and dip variety. A waitress approached us and asked for our drink orders.

"I'll have a Scotch and soda," I said. "What about you, babe?"

"A Coke will be fine for me."

Most of the people appeared younger than our age bracket, some wearing typical business attire, others more casual. Jill checked the crowd to make sure Louie Aregis wasn't among them. Before we reached the snack tables, a smiling young man in a dress shirt and tie but no jacket intercepted us.

"Hi, Greg and Jill, I'm Bob. Welcome to Contacts Nashville. I don't believe you've been with us before. What's your business?"

"McKenzie Investigations," I said. "We're private investigators."

"Great! I think you're the first ones we've had from that field. Circulate around, introduce yourselves, and see if you can't drum up some business. You may already know some of the folks."

I had been checking faces and comparing them to the mental picture of Fred Ricketts I had stored up after studying a photo we'd found online. I turned to Bob.

"Is that Fred Ricketts from P and S Software in the gray suit with the wine-colored tie?"

He looked around. "Right, that's Fred. Want me to introduce you?"

"Sure, if it isn't too much trouble."

"Trouble? You jest. That's what we're here for. Come on."

We followed him to where Ricketts stood beside a table, swishing a chip through a bowl of pale green dip. As I expected, the young man was an imposing figure, even larger than Arnold Wechsel.

"Fred," Bob said, "meet a couple of new folks, Jill and Greg McKenzie of McKenzie Investigations. They're private investigators."

"Nice meeting you," Ricketts said. He dusted his hand with a napkin before reaching out to shake ours. "Don't believe I've met a PI before. I'm afraid all I know about your profession is what I've read in mystery books."

"Then we probably don't fit the picture you have," I said with a grin. "It isn't nearly as exciting and glamorous as the mystery writers would have you believe."

"You're in the software business," Jill said. "We do a lot of our work on the computer. Databases are our bread and butter."

The youthful looking executive nodded. "I hadn't thought of it that way, but I'm sure you're right. Maybe I should look into developing PI software."

The waitress arrived with our drinks. Jill accepted hers and turned back to Ricketts. "You'd find plenty of competition out there. We subscribe to several different databases."

I handed the waitress a ten-dollar bill as I took my glass. "The ones we use have millions of facts about millions of people. You'd be surprised at how much information there is out there, even on people who try hard to leave no trail."

"I can understand that," he said. "Some of my hacker friends in college could dig out about anything you were capable of imagining. And from places you wouldn't think it possible."

I had been sizing up the young man as we talked, and I was impressed. He had alert blue eyes that left the impression they would miss nothing. He seemed to absorb every word and run it through his mental computer in search of a correlation with something that already dwelled there. With the humility of a monk, the smooth delivery of an actor, and the casual familiarity of an old friend, he could have charmed a Scrooge. If this was the man who had stalked us, we faced a formidable opponent.

"I heard you had a passion for auto racing," I said. "Are you involved with the Nashville Superspeedway?"

"No. My interest is solely with IndyCar racing. I'm part-owner of a car on the circuit. We haven't won the Indy 500 yet, but we're hoping."

"I understand that's a pretty pricey sport."

"You're right about that. But it's a thrill a minute."

"Have you done any race driving?"

"Just enough to get hooked on it. I had a friend in college who owned a dragster. I raced it a few times."

I grinned. "That must have really stirred your juices."

He nodded. "Did you know a top fuel dragster can go from zero to 320 miles an hour in under five seconds?"

Jill stared, her eyes widening. "That's unbelievable."

"It's faster acceleration than you'd get in a space shuttle launch," he said.

"We read where you were involved in this effort to bring an NBA team to Nashville," Jill said. "That must be exciting, too."

He shrugged. "We still have a lot of hurdles to jump. I'm excited about the prospects, though. Tell me about what you folks do. What kind of cases do you get involved in?"

I held up my fingers and ticked off a few things. "We handle insurance fraud, particularly involving disability, do background investigations, look for missing persons or missing heirs, work on digging up evidence for attorneys."

"I've always heard PI's went around snooping on cheating spouses."

"We don't get involved in domestic relations," Jill said. "There's enough bitterness in this world without us getting involved in perpetuating it."

"Somehow I find that refreshing," he said as a big man with as big a voice as Ricketts stepped up to greet him.

The newcomer monopolized the conversation, and after a few minutes we moved on to join another group. It was soon time for lunch. Our table proved productive as we met a contractor and a retailer who turned out to be business prospects. We swapped business cards and talked about ways we might be of help, like doing background investigations or tracking down missing property. During the conversation, I mentioned our chat with Fred Ricketts. One of the men told us he was a close friend and had worked with Ricketts on a project for Vanderbilt Children's Hospital.

"Fred knows how to get those kids laughing," he said.

"How does he do it?" Jill asked.

"He's something of an amateur magician."

"What kind of tricks does he do?"

"Simple stuff. Sleight of hand."

"Nothing fancy?" I asked.

"Not with the kids. Now if you want to see fancy tricks, you need to go out to his farm."

"Where's that?"

"Over in Wilson County. He lines up beer cans on the fence and goes down the line—bang, bang, bang! And with a pistol. In the military he'd be a sharpshooter."

I filed that away for future reference.

When the session ended, Jill and I lingered inside until Fred Ricketts headed out to his car.

As we watched, he hurried through the rain straight for the new-looking black Escalade.

19

RATHER THAN MESS with the umbrella, I dashed out to the car, winding up with a cold dousing in the process. I started my Grand Cherokee, which, by comparison to Rickett's Escalade, didn't appear nearly so grand, and pulled up to the covered entrance for Jill.

"Do you think we should add Fred Ricketts to our suspect list?" she asked as she buckled her seatbelt.

"He's a troubling fellow," I said as I headed toward the street. The wipers clacked noisily. The drizzle had mutated into a real shower, and I was surprised it hadn't turned back into snow. "If he was intent on convincing us that he'd never heard of us before, he did a great job as far as I'm concerned."

"I'd have to agree. What about the Cadillac?"

I steered toward the interstate. "As I've often said, I don't believe in coincidences. On the other hand, I'm reluctant to tag him as a suspect based on only one questionable sighting."

"How about the race car angle? Could it have any connection with Arnold Wechsel?"

"I doubt it. Arnold was obsessed with NASCAR. These Indy cars are in a different league. I read where they cost over a million bucks."

"That should separate the men from the boys."

"It would certainly separate the men from their money." I flinched as an eighteen-wheeler passed on the left, kicking a dense shower of water our way. I felt like I was like driving under a waterfall. "The one thing I found troubling was the tale about Ricketts' prowess with a pistol."

"That's certainly a concern," Jill said, "but I'm more bothered by how much credence to put into that casual attitude. Ricketts could've been intentionally misleading us, you know. He'd have made a great Pied Piper. He struck me as a smooth operator in the same class as his colleague, Louie Aregis."

She could be right, but I'd withhold judgment until I had more to go on.

Back at the office, Jill got a call from Wilma Gannon. In contrast to her conversations on our home phone, Wilma always kept it short when using our business line. Jill soon hung up and turned to me.

"We've been invited to dinner at the Gannons."

I looked across at her with a diabolical grin. Since Sam was not the type to put on weight, Wilma never worried about calories.

"That'll be three nights out in a row," I said. "We're on a roll."

"Don't get your mind set on candied yams and yeast rolls and Wilma's chocolate cake. This is a one-night stand. I'll have you back on your low-fat diet tomorrow."

I knew it was time to let that subject drop and turned instead to Nikki Columbo. Since we'd had no word from her, I suggested we head for her Green Hills apartment and have an in-person confrontation. We needed to find something concrete to move our investigation forward.

Before we were ready to leave, however, the phone rang. Red Tarkington.

"I talked to the man I told you about this morning," he said. "The one who says Aregis gypped him out of a lot of money. He found out about it not long before Aregis moved Coastal

Capital Ventures up there. The guy, name's Quillen, is still pretty steamed and wants to talk to you. Said he'd be in Nashville tomorrow. I gave him your number."

"Thanks, Red. We'll be looking for him."

WE TRAVELED THROUGH a cold, steady rain all the way to Green Hills. Nikki's address took us to a vine-covered brick building on a quiet side street. This was an area of older homes in a fashionable section of town that attracted a mix of upwardly mobile young people, successful business types, and retirees. A high-rise for retired teachers was located not far away. I wondered if the vintage structure where Nikki lived might be owned by Zicarelli Properties.

A red Mazda Miata sat in a parking space outside the door to Nikki's apartment.

"It looks like she's here," I said, pulling into an adjacent space. "I'll wait until I see you're inside, then I'll drive over to a coffee shop on Hillsboro Road and wait for you. Call me when you're ready to leave."

"No doughnuts," she said. "Just coffee."

I gave her a peevish frown. "You know you could be charged with cruel and inhuman treatment? You're lucky I don't rat on you to the UN."

She looked like she didn't know whether to laugh or backhand me, but she got out and raised her small, collapsible umbrella. I watched her ring the doorbell. After a moment, the door opened and Nikki Columbo looked out. They exhanged a few words. Following a bit of hesitation, Nikki opened the door wider and Jill stepped inside.

I had high hopes. In situations like this, Jill displayed a motherly demeanor backed by a sincere and understanding attitude that caused people, particularly women, to pour out their hearts. She wasn't judgmental, and she knew when to listen and when to talk. She had been a great interviewer in previous cases.

I found a small coffee shop, ordered coffee and a Danish, a low calorie one, at least in my imagination. I took it to a table that faced a TV tuned to an afternoon news-talk show. A couple of characters with hearsay knowledge of the military argued vehemently about the war on terror. Listening to them, I could almost feel my blood pressure rise.

I was about ready to throw my refill at the TV when the cell phone rang.

"Found your man Izzy," Phil Adamson said.

"Where?"

"One of our guys, Eddie Bledsoe, has an interesting pastime. He drops in on libraries and looks around at who's using the computers. You'd be surprised at what he turns up occasionally. Anyway, this morning he visited the Main Library downtown, and who should he see but Izzy Isabell, pecking away at the keyboard."

"I wish the detective could've gotten on there after Izzy," I said, "and checked out what he'd been doing."

"Hey, if we tried something like that, the librarians would be on us like a flock of mother hens with claws bared."

"You're probably right."

"Detective Bledsoe is a sharp guy, though. He noticed Isabell was writing notes on scratch paper beside the computer. He hung around until the guy got up and left, taking his notes with him. Bledsoe saw a couple of sheets of blank scratch paper lying there. He grabbed them as he followed Isabell out to the parking garage. Made a real score. Got the license number off the truck and turned the note paper over to forensics to see if they could get impressions from what your guy was writing."

Detective work like that was music to my ears. "Gotten any results from it?"

"Not the notes. The Kentucky plate was registered in another name. Hasn't been reported stolen. We've asked Louisville to look into it."

"Let me know what they find," I said. "Meanwhile, I'll keep an eye out for Izzy. I have a crow to pick with him."

I told Phil about the glaring scratch across the side of my Jeep and the note I'd found.

"Too bad they didn't leave a name, so you'd have a witness."

"That's probably not the worst he'll do. From what the parents said about him being on drugs, he's probably gone back to his old habits."

Phil agreed. "I passed along info on him to the folks in narcotics."

When I snapped the cover shut on the phone, I got a missed call alert showing Jill had tried to get me while I was talking to Phil. I called her back.

"I'll be ready by the time you get here," she said, not sounding too pleased.

I hurried out to my Jeep with what coffee was left in the Styrofoam cup and headed for Nikki Columbo's apartment. They must have been standing near the door when I arrived since it opened as soon as I knocked. Nikki's downcast look resembled that of a chastised teen.

"I'm sure everything will work out fine for you," Jill said. "This was a terrible tragedy for everyone. We intend to find out who's responsible. Right, Greg?"

I had no idea where this was going but nodded soberly. "You can count on it."

"I'm sorry if I've disappointed you," Nikki said.

"Call me when you feel like it," Jill said. "Anytime. Bye."

I hurried around to the driver's side to escape the rain. After we were both seated, I looked across at Jill. "That didn't sound too promising."

She gave a deep sigh. "I've never run into one quite like her. When it came to a subject she didn't want to talk about, I couldn't budge her with the sweetest honey in the hive."

"I trust that means you didn't come up with anything startling."

"That's for sure."

"What did she have to say about Arnold?"

"They hadn't been dating for long. They met at the restaurant, as you suspected. He was by himself and looked very lonely. Nikki struck up a conversation and learned that he was from Kaitserslautern. She had studied German in college and spent some time at the University of Tubingen, which is in the state next to the one where Arnold lived."

I drove toward Hillsboro Road, which would take us back to I-440.

"I imagine Nikki knowing his language helped draw him to her," I said.

"I'm sure it did. And she was quite impressed with him. She said Arnold was a determined young man and had his heart set on landing a job in auto racing. There was a school in North Carolina he wanted to attend and was saving his money for it."

"Was that why he wanted an extra job?"

"Apparently. But she wouldn't talk about his job. She got real defensive, said it was something personal."

"With a background in German studies, I presume she's had a problem finding a job in her field. That why she's working at a restaurant?"

A pickup truck roared out of a side street and slashed across three lanes of traffic in front of us. I hit the antilock brakes and gave thanks we didn't go into a skid. My first thought was Izzy Isabell, but the truck wasn't blue. If it hadn't been for the seatbelt, Jill would've gone airborne. She reached out to the dash to steady herself.

"What an idiot! And in this rain." She exhaled like a hiss of steam. "At times like this I have to agree that Nashville drivers must be the world's worst."

I waved a hand. "I'll not argue the point. But let's get back to Nikki."

Jill pulled her seatbelt tighter. "She said Villa de Este was a temporary job until she could find something that would make use of her German abilities."

"What did she say about the Zicarelli connection?"

"She started to deny knowing anything about it until I told her we knew her mother was Belinda Zicarelli. I said I imagined she had relatives here. She didn't want to talk about it but slipped up once and mentioned 'Grandpa.' I presume it would have to be Grandpa Zicarelli as there are no Columbos around here."

"Did she exhibit any of that fear we saw last night?"

"Not so much fear as a deep concern about giving out personal information. She's definitely holding something back."

"Hopefully we can figure a way to get it out of her. It sounded like you parted on a friendly basis."

"I was very sympathetic about her loss and tried to comfort her. She's a confused young lady at the moment."

As I merged into the traffic on I-440, known locally as the Outer Loop, I got a strange feeling that we were being followed. I searched the mirror for any familiar vehicles. With the afternoon's thick clouds leaving a darkened haze and poor visibility from the rain, it was a difficult task. Nothing raised any alarms, but I couldn't shake that odd premonition.

20

NOT LONG AFTER we made it back to the office, my Realtor friend called.

"I found the owner of Zicarelli Properties," she said. "His name is Niccolo Zicarelli. I hear he goes by the name Nick. Italian, obviously."

"Know anything else about him?" I asked.

"Just that he owns several pieces of commercial property around town. Investment property. Some pretty good sized investments."

I thanked her and relayed the information to my partner.

"It has to be her grandpa," Jill said. "She must have been named for him. Nicole is the female version of Niccolo. I'll check the databases."

She punched the name in on one of our high-powered search sites and soon had a few interesting facts. Nick Zicarelli, age eighty-one, once owned a private club known as the Sporting Executives Club in the northwestern suburbs of Nashville. For the past quarter century he had been involved in real estate investments and was reputed to be a professional gambler. There was no record of him having served any jail time.

"The newspaper should have plenty on him," Jill said. "Why don't you call Wes Knight?"

I figured Wes might have the answer without looking in the files. He had as many gray hairs as I did. He'd started with the newspaper about the time I signed on as a St. Louis County deputy just out of the University of Michigan, my warm-up for the Air Force. I got the reporter on the phone and told him I was looking for information on Nick Zicarelli.

"It's a good thing you asked an old timer like me, Greg. The young ones probably wouldn't have any idea who he really is. Forty years ago, he was quite a colorful character around town. Tall and good looking."

"I ran across something about a Sporting Executives Club."

"That was his baby. He started out as a waiter there, married the boss's daughter, and soon took over. It was a great place to eat and drink and do a little gambling."

"Wasn't that slightly illegal? How did he stay out of trouble?"

"His heyday was back before the advent of Metropolitan Government. The club was located outside the city limits, so all he had to worry about was the sheriff."

"And he didn't really have to worry about the sheriff," I said.

"You've got it. Zicarelli helped them get elected and provided free drinks and meals. It was a hangout for lawyers and judges and cops, among others."

"Sounds like a cozy deal."

"It was. I understand they used to have some pretty high stakes poker games at the tables."

"What happened?"

"Metro eventually wrecked his little red wagon."

"That's when the police department took over the whole county?"

"Right. Things didn't change overnight, of course. The heat eventually got to him, though. He tried to go legit, but the place had lost its charm. He eventually closed it down in the seventies."

I glanced at my note from the Realtor. "He must have done pretty well. I hear he owns a lot of commercial real estate around town."

"Yeah, he made a small fortune off that club. I've heard he's still involved in gambling, but on a more discreet basis. Nothing like the old days. Now he's Mr. Nice Guy. He gives money to all the favorite causes, and he's still pals with the politicos. That's the face the younger reporters see."

"Did he come over from Italy?"

"No, he's a local boy. As I recall, he was a standout basketball player in high school. Instead of getting ready for college, though, he dropped out of school and joined the Army after Pearl Harbor. He got some commendations in Europe. I remember he was cited for shooting a bunch of Germans in some battle. Hometown hero, y'know."

I thanked Wes and repeated the conversation for Jill.

She tapped a pencil on her desk with a look that told me the wheels were turning rapidly inside. "The story sounds sort of familiar now. I don't believe my dad patronized such places, but he may have sold him insurance. Maybe Nick Zicarelli had been giving Arnold advice on gambling, which Nikki didn't approve of."

"That could account for her reluctance to talk about the relationship."

She brushed the idea aside along with a lock of black hair. "But it doesn't give us any hint of who killed Arnold Wechsel, or why."

I thought about that for a moment. Dick Ullery talked about Arnold going places and meeting people while working at this mystery job. What if his mother's suspicions were correct, that somehow gambling had been involved? And what if Arnold had been contacting these people about bets, collecting money or making payoffs?

"Maybe we could get some insight into what Arnold was up to if we contacted one of those people Ullery told us about," I said.

"Like the TV pitchman, Freddie Ford?"

"Right. He's full of himself on his commercials. Let's go see how he does off-camera."

"You don't suppose his name is really Ford, do you?"

"Why not? He could have made it Ford for advertising purposes. Maybe I should go to court and change my name to P.I. McKenzie."

The look I got said that idea wasn't worth the effort it took to express it.

WITH THE FIRST phase of homebound traffic clogging the outbound lanes of I-40, we had no trouble making our way toward town where the Ford dealership was located just off an interstate exit. The rain had finally stopped, but eighteen-wheelers still tossed nasty showers our way as they passed. We turned in beside a monstrous Ford logo sign and pulled up to the dome-shaped building. It was clearly a monument to the man we had come to see. In the showroom we faced a larger-than-life poster of Freddie Ford with his finger pointing in an "Uncle Sam wants YOU!" gesture.

I stopped at the Customer Service counter, where a young woman wearing a heavy wool sweater tidied up her desk. "We'd like to see Freddie Ford, please," I said.

"Could one of the salesmen help you?" she asked in an eager voice no doubt reserved for prospective customers.

"It isn't about a car. It's a personal matter."

"Oh. Let me see if he's available. Could I have your name, please?"

"Greg and Jill McKenzie," I said.

She picked up her phone, punched in a number, and spoke

too softly for me to hear. She put down the phone and nodded toward a hallway. "You can go on back to his office. It's the last room on the left."

We passed an empty office and another that appeared to be the torture chamber, the place where the sales manager browbeat customers who had the temerity to think they could negotiate a rock-bottom deal on one of Freddie's new Fords.

A large, flat-screen TV dominated the owner's office. I presumed he enjoyed watching himself perform. A short, stocky man with lively eyes and a quick smile, he spoke in the strong tones of a carnival barker.

"Come in, folks." He bounded around the desk. "Welcome to Freddie Ford."

He pumped our hands with a strong grip, and I half-expected him to launch into one of his familiar sales pitches.

"We're Greg and Jill McKenzie," I said, handing him our card. "We're private investigators. Do you recall reading or seeing about a young man named Arnold Wechsel who was shot over in Northeast Nashville last Saturday night?"

He backtracked to brace his hands against his desk, frowning. "Arnold Wechsel? Did he used to work for us? The name doesn't sound familiar."

I tried a disarming smile. "A friend of his told us he was quite excited about meeting you recently. He was a young German, a big guy, six feet tall." I held up a hand to mark his height.

"Sorry," he said, shaking his head.

"His mother in Germany asked us to find out anything we can about his life over here. According to his friend, Arnold met you in some kind of business relationship."

His face brightened. "I probably sold him a car. Frankly, I sell so many I can't remember all the buyers. You'd be surprised at how many I sold just this past week."

"No, he didn't buy a car."

"You sure?"

"He drove an old model Corvette. I believe he talked to you about a betting matter."

He cut his eyes toward me, then Jill. "I don't know nothing about that."

Jill spoke in a quiet voice. "Was Arnold Wechsel collecting a gambling debt from you, Mr. Ford?"

He looked shocked. I'm sure he hadn't expected that coming from her.

"No!" he shouted after a telling pause. He turned toward the doorway in an obvious effort to be rid of us. "I'm sorry, I have to go check with my staff before closing."

21

WE BYPASSED the office and drove straight home to freshen up before heading for the Gannons. Our brief interview with Freddie Ford left us more than ever convinced that Arnold had been a party to some sort of gambling activity. Whether it involved Nick Zicarelli was less certain. We needed to do more digging on that score.

When we arrived at our friends' house, the unmistakable aroma of seafood greeted us. Wilma brought out plates heaped with shrimp, scallops, and strips of flounder along with steaming, buttery baked potatoes. A green salad tossed with balsamic vinaigrette and parmesan croutons rounded out the meal, and she had made fudge brownies, my favorite. I watched carefully to time my plate refills with moments when Jill turned her head to talk with our hostess. Sam grinned like a chimp as he watched my little game.

After dinner, we adjourned to the den, Sam and I with our coffee mugs. The room had a bit more of a homey look than two nights ago. Fewer candles danced about and comfortable, casual furniture replaced the long table and folding chairs. Sam had gone by the church this morning to return the chairs and encountered the preacher, who apologized for missing our class party.

"He also wanted to know if our favorite snoopers had gone AWOL," Sam said, looking across at me.

Jill and I had missed the last two Sundays. She'd flown us

down to Ft. Lauderdale in her Cessna a couple of weeks ago for a consultation with a PI friend and a few days of R&R. This past Sunday we were mired deep in the Wechsel murder and Terry Tremont's case.

"What did you tell him?" I asked, fearing the worst.

Sam gave a twinkle-eyed shrug. "I told him if he read the papers he should've known you'd be out tracking down a murderer."

"I can imagine his comeback." The good reverend loved to needle me.

"He said he'd noticed you spent a lot of time looking for bodies these days."

"Dr. Trent sounds more like our favorite homicide detective, Phil Adamson," Jill said.

I didn't know she'd been listening, but I agreed. "Those homicide guys have a good reason for making jokes about their cases. It keeps them from going bonkers over all the blood and gore."

"After that comment, I leveled with the preacher," Sam said with a shake of his head. "I told him you'd been to Florida. He said that was an acceptable excuse. Just don't miss this Sunday."

Following that bit of repartee, Wilma and Jill began to take apart the state of education in the public schools, and Sam brought me up to date on his basketball-playing Dollar Deal friend.

"He says his boss is concerned about Aregis's grandstanding," Sam said. "He thinks they'd be better off keeping things a little more low-key until they have something positive to announce."

I sipped at my coffee, debating a refill, as I digested that observation. "Sounds like there might be a bit of disharmony in the ranks."

"He didn't get specific, but I got the feeling Howard Hays wasn't real happy with the way Aregis has been acting."

"Hays is the most prominent party in the group," I said. "He doesn't want anything to go wrong that would reflect on his reputation or that of his company. Did it sound like a serious disagreement, like they night be souring on the deal?"

"Oh, no. My friend is still all pumped up over the prospects. He's really looking forward to it."

"Has he mentioned any teams they're courting?"

Sam leaned back and laced his fingers behind his head. "Not that I recall. He said earlier that they were looking at several prospects."

"I guess it all boils down to finding a team owner who's willing to consider selling."

"Would your client be happy if they can't find one?" Sam asked.

I set my coffee mug on the small table between us and smiled. "True. Personally, I'm not too concerned about whether or not we get an NBA team here, but I damned sure want to know who killed a man who called me and wanted to talk about it."

"Greg!"

Jill caught me off guard, though I realized I had raised my voice a bit. And I knew I shouldn't have said what I said. I was getting a bit touchy over the lack of progress in finding who had killed Arnold.

"Sorry, babe," I said. "I'll watch my tongue."

"You'd better, if you don't want me to wash your mouth out with soap."

"Yes, mom," I said, and grinned.

Wilma caught my attention with a wave. "You know you two are invited over Saturday for Christmas dinner. Tara will be here with the grandsons."

Tara was the widow of the Gannons' son, Tim, whose murder we had solved down at Perdido Key a year ago. It was the event that prompted us to go into the PI business.

"The way this case is going," I said, "I'm hesitant to make any commitments. There's no telling when something might break and we could suddenly find ourselves ankle deep in alligators."

WE LEFT THE Gannons' at nine o'clock. The clouds had broken up, freeing the ground heat to fritter away and the temperature to dip below freezing. The formerly wet streets now showed icy spots beneath a bright gibbous moon, which bathed nearby lawns in its pale glow. The gusty wind had died down. I turned on the heater to clear a few frosty patches from the windshield.

I swung onto Chandler Road and headed for the McKenzie spread. Traffic was light, almost non-existent. We oohed and aahed at the houses with strings of glittering lights and yards decorated with Christmas scenes. That was one chore I didn't have to worry about, since our house was invisible from the street. Some lawns featured mangers and shepherds, while others spotlighted a jolly old gent in a sleigh pulled by reindeer. Closer to home, my mind wandered to the Cadillac Escalade from Sunday night and the question of whether it could be related to Arnold Wechsel's murder.

I dismissed the thought as I pulled into our driveway. The landscape appeared quiet and peaceful, but about halfway into the wooded area, the headlights picked out a box large enough to hold a basketball. It sat just off the driveway. I slowed and stared.

"Where did that thing come from?" I pointed it out to Jill.

She leaned forward in her seat. "Maybe it fell off a delivery truck."

"Possibly, but delivery trucks don't usually go around with their doors open in back. I'll check it out."

"Don't bother it if it looks suspicious."

"I won't."

I eased the car forward. As I was about to stop, a blast rocked us. The front end of the Jeep reared up like a bucking bronco. I felt my body slammed back against the seat. The thunderous roar was deafening. My head seemed about to split. A second jolt shook me as the vehicle fell back to the driveway.

I thought I'd been blinded. Then I stared and realized the lights had gone out.

"Jill...babe!"

I reached for her frantically. She hadn't made a sound.

My thoughts were a jumble? What had happened? Was she badly hurt? I remembered the void it left in my life when she was abducted two years ago.

I felt her arm move and grabbed her hand.

"Greg?" Her voice sounded weak to my ringing ears.

"Are you hurt?" I could see only a dim outline in the dark.

"I think...I must have...must have bumped my head."

I realized my left leg hurt and vaguely recalled something hitting it during the chaos.

"Something banged my leg," I said. "Does anything hurt besides your head?"

"I don't think so." She sounded a bit clearer. "What happened?"

I looked out the broken windshield and saw the hood up and twisted to the side. It looked like we'd been hit by a mortar. The windshield had disintegrated into small particles of glass scattered about, nothing large enough to cause an injury. Turning to the window, I spotted pieces of debris scattered about in the moonlight. As I clawed the cobwebs away from my head, I realized what had happened.

"It was an explosion," I said. "Some kind of bomb is all I can think of."

"A bomb?"

A pungent odor jerked me upright.

Gasoline.

I hit the seat belt release and leaned across to press Jill's. "Get out of here before this thing goes up in flames!" I yelled.

22

I WATCHED AS Jill opened the door and slid out. The blast had occurred up front on my side. I wasn't sure what damage it might have done. I grabbed the door handle and slammed my shoulder just below the window, praying it would open. With a crunch, the door swung to the side. I bounded out and ran around the back, yelling at Jill to call 911. Reaching the other side, I found the door ajar where she had jumped out. I reached in and probed under the dash for the fire extinguisher I kept stashed against the frame.

The Jeep suddenly shuddered with a loud whoomp! Jill's high-pitched scream sent me dancing backward. I saw flames leap above the engine compartment. My hand clutched the extinguisher, but I knew it was too small to fight a fire like this.

I grabbed Jill by the hand and almost dragged her down the driveway toward the street. Smoke boiled up and flames brightened the area as if somebody had lit a huge bonfire. I held her tightly, noticed the upper lip curled between her teeth as we watched in awe, totally absorbed by the pyrotechnic display.

I thought of my initial reaction that it must have been a bomb. In our driveway? Who could have put it there, and why? Was it former Lt. Izzy Isabell? I recalled the box in the grass. Had it been placed there as a lure, intended to make me slow down or stop? The troubling events of the past few nights painted a confusing picture. I had ruled out Isabell as responsible for the SUV parked nearby in the street. And this was multiple times more serious than a scratch on the side of the car. Did that mean it was related to the Wechsel murder? The phone call while we were gone, and the intrusion that set off the outside floodlights last night could have been anybody. It left a garbled picture. Was this meant as a warning, or did somebody want us dead?

Sirens blaring in the distance abruptly broke my concentration. I squeezed Jill more tightly. "It sounds like help is on the way, babe."

The moonlight was enough to show the distress in her eyes. "Who could have done this, Greg?"

"I don't know, but we'd better figure it out before they succeed in whatever they're after."

Headlight beams swung into the driveway, highlighting the blazing Cherokee. I turned to see the psychedelic display of red lights as the fire truck rumbled toward us. More lights followed, apparently from a Metro ambulance. The firefighters jumped off the truck and swarmed around us. I heard more sirens in the distance.

"Is that your car?" asked a fireman who seemed to be in charge.

"What's left of it," I said.

"You reported a bomb?"

"That's right. It exploded under the front of my Jeep."

"Were you in it?"

"My wife and I were. We got out before the fire started."

Another siren entered our driveway. I glanced back and saw one of the smaller vehicles driven by district chiefs.

"Were either of you injured?" the fireman asked.

My leg felt sore, but in all the confusion I hadn't bothered to check the aftermath of whatever had hit me. I looked down and saw a tear in my pants leg.

"A piece of metal apparently hit my leg," I said, pulling up my pants.

A paramedic from the ambulance had walked up and shined his flashlight toward my foot. It showed a cut that left the top of my sock a soggy red.

"You're going to need some stitches," he said.

Frustrated at my inability to have any impact on the situation, I stared at the heavily-clad firemen standing around. "Are you going to put the fire out?"

"Nobody goes close to it until the HazMat crew gets here," one of them said. "There may be explosives that haven't detonated."

The paramedic had been examining my leg. "Come on back to the unit and let me clean that up. We need to get both of you to Summit ER and let them check you out. There could be internal damage."

I'd been in wrecks with more shock than this that didn't cause internal damage, but I'd deal with that later. The medic, a lanky fellow in uniform coveralls with a solicitous bedside manner, took me by the arm and led me to his ambulance. Jill followed us. On the way, we encountered the district chief.

"HazMat should be here any minute," he said. "What's the situation?"

"The situation is my Jeep is toast," I said. "Why do you need HazMat?"

He gave me a look reserved for the uninformed. "They'll have to check it out for anything hazardous before we can turn the investigators loose."

More sirens pierced the cold night air as the blue lights of a Metro police car pulled in, followed by another fire engine and a ladder truck. You'd have thought we'd been under siege by terrorists. I suppose that's what they were assuming.

The chief hurried on up to where the firemen stood, and

the paramedic began working on my leg. Moments later we were joined by a Metro cop wearing sergeant's stripes. He was short and stocky, in his forties. I recognized him immediately, Sgt. Gerald Christie. He pushed his cap back to show a receding hairline.

"Looks like you have a problem, Mr. McKenzie." His tone resembled a taunt more than a concern.

"Just a small one, Sergeant Christie," I said. "The Fire Department is taking care of it very well, as you can see."

The officer smiled. "I'll go see what the Police Department can do to help."

My one and only encounter with the sergeant had come two years earlier when local affiliates of a Palestinian terrorist group ransacked our house and took Jill hostage. After noting that he obviously enjoyed my misery, I learned he was the brother-in-law of Murder Squad Detective Mark Tremaine. The detective had unmercifully tormented John Peterson, a young husband whose wife, Tessa, had disappeared, ignoring other possible suspects. It led to my supposedly off-the-record diatribe that appeared on page one of the morning paper, ending my brief investigative career with the District Attorney's office.

He walked toward the firemen as the paramedic finished patching up my leg.

Jill frowned, her gaze following the sergeant. "Is that the man you told me about after the scroll affair?"

"That's jolly old Saint Gerald, Mrs. Tremaine's brother."

"He didn't sound too concerned," the paramedic said as he completed the tape job.

"We aren't exactly friends," I said. "His only concern is that I suffer enough."

"I'd better get you folks to the ER," the medic said. He squatted and shoved his first aid paraphernalia into the bag.

"Thanks," I said, "but that won't be necessary."

"You need some stitches."

"My wife can take me later. I appreciate your concern, but we're private investigators. We need to find out what's going on here."

"If you decline to let us transport you to the hospital, you'll have to sign a release," he said.

I turned to Jill. "You're okay, aren't you?"

"I'm fine," she said, "but you need that leg looked into."

"It'll be okay until things are wrapped up here."

Sergeant Christie returned as I was signing the release.

"Looks like you have a nice pile of rubble decorating your driveway," he said. "I've called for a couple of officers to keep people away from the scene."

I ignored him. A few people from the neighborhood had gathered out in the street, but the HazMat team's arrival kept them from trying to get any closer. Jill and I walked back to where the district chief stood. I heard one of the firemen yelling and saw two people coming through the trees that separated our property from the neighbor next door. I recognized Jay Rogers and his son, Ricky.

"It's okay," I called out. "They're my neighbors."

The fireman herded them over to where we stood. A tall, lanky man with long arms apparently made for swinging a tennis racket, Jay looked across at the debris.

"Are you two okay?" he asked, showing genuine compassion in contrast to Sergeant Christie's blasé attitude.

"Just a little cut on my leg" I said. "Jill bumped her head. We got out before the fire started."

"It made one heck of a blast. I was in the shower and thought we'd had an earthquake. What happened?"

"I wish I knew. Something exploded under the front of the Jeep. Then it caught fire."

"Sheesh! It's sure lucky you got out when you did. Anything we can do to help?"

"Did you see any cars or trucks over here tonight?" I asked. "Anything that might have looked strange?"

Jay cocked his head thoughtfully. "It would've had to be back in the cleared area for me to see anything. I didn't hear anything, either."

I patted him on the shoulder. "Thanks anyway, Jay. I think everything's under control. We can use Jill's car until I get a chance to find a new one. That Jeep had seen its better days."

It had survived a battering down in Orange Beach a year ago and wound up with a new paint job. Now it lay beyond redemption, nothing left but a smoldering chassis. Izzy Isabell's defacing scratch was nothing but a memory. Losing my faithful Jeep hit me almost like losing a loyal hunting dog, but what I felt at whoever had put Jill and me in jeopardy was pure outrage. I wanted to track him down and make him pay.

First I had to deal with the here and now. The chief insisted that Jay and Ricky move out to the street. I didn't think it was necessary since the flames appeared to be dying out around my Jeep. However, the bulky-suited hazardous materials specialists remained clustered nearby.

When my cell phone rang, I pulled it off my belt and answered.

"What the hell's going on, Greg?" Phil Adamson asked. "One of the guys called and said there'd been an explosion at your house."

"Unfortunately true. My Jeep is among the dearly departed."

His voice turned cautious. "Anybody hurt? What happened?"

I told him about our minor injuries and my speculation regarding a bomb.

"Jeez. You think it had to do with that Cadillac Escalade?"

"That or Izzy Isabell, but who knows?"

"Without a tag number or model year, tracking down that Caddy would be like taking the haystack apart straw by straw to find the needle."

"And you don't have the manpower for haystack dismantling."

"You've got that right."

"From all the fire equipment around here, even a HazMat team, you'd think we'd been attacked by Osama bin Laden."

"That's standard procedure when there's a bomb report."

I changed the subject. "Anything new on the Wechsel case?" I hoped something positive might be salvaged from this ill-starred night.

He was silent a moment as if debating his reply. "The computer guys determined that he had used software to scrub his hard drive of anything he didn't want found. But there was one file he either hadn't finished or forgot about. It looked like a draft of a letter. No name, no address, no salutation. Indicated he felt he'd been treated unfairly. Said he thought he had done as instructed. The fact he didn't come back with the money wasn't his fault."

The other job we'd heard about? "Anything else in it?"

"The tone changed toward the end. Apparently he'd been fired, and he sounded really pissed."

I looked across at my Jeep, which appeared to be barely smoldering. "The people we talked to said Arnold was prone to outbursts of anger," I said.

"That's the picture we got, too."

"But the letter gave no indication who it was directed to?"

"None."

"Could it be the killer?"

"That's a possibility. It wasn't anybody at the race car shop, though. He was still working there. When I talked to them, they sounded highly complimentary."

"I hope you can find out who it involved," I said. My peripheral vision caught a stir among the HazMat crew. "We're waiting for the fire investigator to come. I'll let you know what he turns up."

23

AFTER I'D PUNCHED off the phone, I began to wonder if the intended recipient of Arnold's letter could be the person who had set off a bomb beneath my Jeep. If that was the case, he must believe we were getting close to identifying him. Too bad I didn't have that kind of confidence.

Jill leaned toward me and spoke in a soft voice. "Hadn't we better get you checked out at the Emergency Room?"

The ambulance had left for another call. I looked around. "I don't know that we could get past this road block. Anyway, I want to see what the fire investigator finds."

"Might have known you'd be stubborn about it," she said, a grim look on her face.

"Come on, babe. You want to know what's going on here as much as I do."

"Yes, but I don't want you getting an infection in that leg."

"The medic cleaned it good and put an antibiotic on it. I'm fine." I put on a false face to mask the pain I tried to ignore.

The HazMat crew had just decided there was no further danger when the investigator arrived. He appeared to be fortyish, with a straight slash of a mouth and a square jaw that gave him a determined look. He spoke to the district chief, then walked over to us.

"I understand you were in the vehicle," he said.

"Right." I introduced Jill and myself and explained up front that we were private investigators.

His eyes appeared to give me a little more contemplative look and he held out his hand. "Buddy Ebsen. No relation to Jed Clampett. Tell me exactly what happened."

I detailed our arrival and the shocking explosion.

"This happened before the fire?"

"Definitely," I said. "My guess is a ruptured gas line leaked fuel onto the hot engine block."

"Or possibly the catalytic converter. They generate quite a bit of heat. If you're private investigators, are you working on a case that might have triggered this?"

Actually, I had questions about its relation to the NBA affair, but I decided to attack it indirectly. "I was involved in something last Saturday night that might be connected."

I told him about Arnold Wechsel's murder. He recalled reading the news story.

"I asked Chief Yunker to have the policemen knock on doors around the neighborhood and find out if anyone saw anything out of the ordinary. Let me make some photos, then I'll take a look around."

Jill and I watched as he removed a digital camera from his case and made a calculated circuit of the remains, snapping dozens of photos. He put the camera away and used a flashlight with a powerful beam to probe about the front of the vehicle. Returning to his equipment case, he pulled out a device that looked a bit like a Dustbuster.

He looked across at me, knowing I'd be curious. "This is a bomb sniffer machine. It'll detect what kind of explosive was used. I don't usually carry it with me, but it was handy so I brought it along."

He moved back around to where a large hole in the driveway marked the location of the explosion. After aiming the odd-looking device around the area, he checked the read-out.

"Just as I suspected. ANFO."

"What's that stand for?"

"Ammonium nitrate and fuel oil. The favorite materials for IED's in Iraq and Afghanistan, most famously used to blow up the Murrah Federal Building in Oklahoma City."

"And readily available anywhere around Nashville," I said.

"Your attacker wasn't skilled at this, or you'd be no better off than your car. If the ingredients aren't mixed in exactly the correct proportion, the explosive effects won't be as powerful as intended."

I looked at the metal skeleton, all that was left of my Jeep. "Glad we have something to be thankful for."

He reached for his cell phone. "I need to call for a wrecker and get this hauled off to our forensic lab downtown. We'll scour it for any kind of trace evidence. I'll check with the ATF and be back to comb the area in the morning."

Jill had called Wilma Gannon while I followed Ebsen's probe of the fire scene. She and Sam drove up about the time the investigator finished. My leg wasn't too happy with the way I had ignored it, so I made no objection to their offer to drive us to the Emergency Room. The hospital was only a few miles away on Old Hickory Boulevard.

With the clock getting on toward midnight, accidents on the icy roads had brought more than the normal crowd of patients. We found seating scarce as clumps of concerned families and friends crowded the waiting room. I was shuffled back to a small treatment room where they had me stretch out on one of those comfort-defying beds. Jill gave lip service to my plight, but I knew she was secretly satisfied that I got what I deserved. When the doctor finally got around to me, he took Jill's side and chewed me out for not coming in sooner. His sewing job didn't feel as gentle as my mother's technique in darning socks had appeared, but I suffered through it, got bandaged up, and joined Jill and the Gannons for the drive home.

The remains of my Jeep had been hauled away by the time we got there. The hole in the driveway and a large area around it had been marked off with crime scene tape. Sam maneuvered around it and dropped us off at the house.

"Anything else we can do for you?" he asked as we got out.

"Thanks," I said, no doubt sounding as weary as I felt. "You've already gone way above and beyond. Get on home and hit the sack before it's time for the alarm to go off."

"The only alarm Sam knows about is the one that goes off on the weather radio," Wilma said. "He probably won't get up until you're at the office."

Sam shrugged. "Don't call early or you'll find her in bed, too. You probably need to get a little extra rest yourself, Greg."

"If I don't get to work on time, my partner might dock my pay," I said.

Jill reached over to pat my stomach. "I'll dock your dinner plate if you don't shape up."

When we got in the house, we found a message on the answering machine. Wes Knight wanted me to call him at the newspaper. I glanced at my watch. Way past their deadline. I knew it was safe to punch in the number.

"You have reached the desk of Wesley Knight. Please leave a message and I'll get back to you as soon as possible."

I smiled. "Hey, Wes. This is Greg McKenzie. I got a cut on my leg and had to languish in the Emergency Room for a while. Just got home. I guess you know something exploded under my Jeep's bumper. If you can get anything out of the Fire Department, you'll know more than I do."

I placed the phone onto its base and turned to Jill. I felt like I'd been wrung out and hung out. "Let's call it a day, babe. Or a night. Or maybe a week."

24

THE PAIN IN MY leg had diminished little if any by the next morning. It only added to my determination to track down whoever was responsible for the annihilation of my Jeep, as well as the threat to my wife, and possibly the murder of Arnold Wechsel. The newspaper included a brief mention of the explosion "of unknown origin" that still besmirched a sizeable section of our driveway. The story said no one was seriously injured. I had to agree, it could have been a lot worse if we hadn't bailed out when we did. That hardly lessened the soreness of my stitched-up leg.

After arriving at the office in Jill's Camry, we replied to a few emails inquiring about the news item, including one from our insurance agent. We discussed what to do about alternate transportation while drinking our cappuccino.

"Do you want another Jeep?" Jill asked.

"I haven't made up my mind," I said. "It makes a good car for a PI. Not flashy, but not monstrous like some SUV's. Has space for hauling equipment. Yet it's decent enough to take for a night on the town."

She narrowed her eyes. "When have we had a night on the town?"

"You've forgotten about Red Lobster after the symphony?"

"Oh, horrors, how could I have forgotten that?"

"And the dancing..."

"Dancing?"

"Remember those lobsters shimmying around in the tank?"

She turned back to her computer, shaking her head.

VERNON QUILLEN of Pensacola called to see if we were in. He was at the Music City Sheraton Hotel near the airport and said he would be here in fifteen minutes. He arrived right on time.

About Jill's height, some would call it average, he wore a heavy tan jacket but no hat. Looking at his polished dome, I wondered if his mama had told him he'd lose most of his body heat through that egg-shaped expanse of skin? That's what I'd always believed until I read where research showed it was a myth. In striking contrast, his broad mouth was circled by a black goatee. It gave him a sinister look.

I moved around my desk to greet him. "Mr. Quillen?"

"Vernon," he said, reaching out his hand.

"I'm Greg. Are you in town on business?"

"Among other things. I own a charter bus company and work closely with a firm up here. I'd been meaning to pay them a visit ever since we suffered all the hurricane damage back in September."

I introduced Jill and invited him to have a seat in one of the client chairs that faced my desk. "Sorry we don't have a little more Florida-like weather for you," I said.

"It's been pretty chilly in Pensacola. Not quite this bad, though. Your private investigator friend said you were interested in Louie Aregis."

"We are. What can you tell us about him?"

Quillen unzipped his jacket and crossed a leg as he straightened up in the chair. "The bastard, if I may use the appropriate term"—he glanced apologetically at Jill—"took me for two hundred and fifty thousand dollars."

"Recently?"

"I just discovered it a few months ago."

"How'd it happen?"

"He sold me on putting money into a new business he was helping get started. He runs a venture capital firm, you know."

"What sort of business?"

"Solar power. With all the sunshine Florida talks about, it sounded like a natural."

"Didn't turn out that way?"

"In a word, a big fat 'no.'"

"And you lost a quarter of a million dollars?"

"Yeah. Money I didn't need to lose."

"Did the company go under?"

"With a thud. Obviously, Aregis didn't do his due diligence. He claims he lost money on the deal, too, but I'm not so sure of that. I know he got his commission on my part of it."

Jill came over and stood beside my desk. "Would you have any recourse to get your money back?" she asked.

"I talked to my lawyer. He says unless we can prove that Aregis intentionally deceived me or failed to inform me of some material fact that put me at more than normal risk, I'm not likely to have any luck."

I shuffled around in a file folder to find the data search results on Louie Aregis. "Have you done any background checking on the man since he did this to you?"

Quillen folded his arms. "I didn't hire anybody, if that's what you mean."

"On your own?"

"I looked into his lavish lifestyle. He had a fancy home on the bay not far from the Pensacola Country Club. It took a big hit from the hurricane, but he'd already left. His wife was the belle of the ball, her picture always showing up somewhere. I don't run in those circles, but I have a few friends who do. I asked around."

When he paused, I prodded him. "What was their reaction?"

"They viewed him as a shifty character. They'd take his money if he wanted to buy something, but they weren't about to give him any of theirs. Wish I'd talked to them first."

"Did anybody get specific about it?"

"One thing, I don't know if anybody had any solid information, but they said his mother's family in Miami had Mafia connections."

"Interesting," I said. "We hadn't heard that."

"What are you folks after him for?"

"We're looking into his relationship with a deal to bring an NBA team to Nashville."

"Crap. I wouldn't touch that with a pair of ten-foot poles."

"He's got some pretty big guns behind him," Jill said.

Quillen gave a disgusted shake of his bald head. "If they're smart, they'll use the guns to blow off his lying head."

Shortly after Quillen left, Buddy Ebsen, the fire investigator with the famous name, called. "I'm over at your place with an ATF agent, Mr. McKenzie. We've found evidence that someone may have hidden in the wooded area at one side of your driveway. He could've waited there and triggered the explosion. There's a trail through the trees that leads out to the road. He likely parked his car in a smooth area across the street that may have been a driveway or access road at one time. According to the police, nobody saw anything, though."

"I know the place you're talking about. Somebody started to build a house over there a couple of years ago, then changed his mind. We have to complain to codes now and then to get the weeds cut."

"If the guy who did this parked over there, he didn't leave any evidence of what he drove. The area's graveled, so there were no tire tracks."

"Did you turn up anything along the trail?"

"Yeah. Near where our man must have hidden, we found a piece of white tape with handwriting on it. My ATF buddy says it contains a designation that indicates it came off `a mobile ham radio transceiver."

"Could a radio have been used to trigger the explosion?"

"That's exactly what I think happened. We looked for cell phone debris but didn't find any. He could have used a very small receiver to trigger the detonator that would have been destroyed by the explosion. One tuned to the frequency he used on his handheld. Do you know any ham radio operators?"

"Nobody comes to mind. What about that box beside the driveway? Did you learn anything from it?"

"No. It was a generic corrugated box you can buy at any office supply store. It had no writing on it. No contamination from explosives, except for being blown several yards away. Also no fingerprints. It could have been used as a lure, but I'd say the guy was careful enough to wear gloves."

"Are you through with the scene? Is it okay to fill the hole in the driveway?"

"Sure. We've got all we need."

"Thanks for calling," I said. "Let me know if you find anything else. Okay?"

"I'll do what I can, Mr. McKenzie. Call me if you thank of any connection with a ham radio operator. It's a long shot, but you never know when something like that might pay off."

"What's the story?" Jill asked when I put the phone down.

I repeated what the investigator had told me.

"Does any of that match with what you know about Lieutenant Isabell?"

"No," I said. "I never heard anything about him being involved in amateur radio."

"Do you think they might find additional clues from the wreckage?"

"I would hope so, but don't count on it."

"What's next?"

"Why don't you give Nikki a call? See if you can coax something else out of her with what we learned about Nick Zicarelli."

She picked up her phone, and I turned to my computer, experiencing a return of that uneasy feeling about Arnold Wechsel. There was something about him that I was missing. Something important. What it could be still stumped me. I decided to try the old routine that had worked well in the past. Rather than use the computer, I took out pen and pad and began listing major points in the investigation. It started with finding the body at the repair shop. I added the visit with Pete Lara, the talk with Wechsel's neighbor, the questioning of Richard Ullery, right down to the identification of Nick Zicarelli. I had begun to look for common threads among the information we had gathered when I heard Jill approach my desk.

I looked around to see a troubled look on her face. "Problems?" I asked.

"I'm hardly making any progress with Nikki."

"What did she say about grandpa?"

"She admitted we were right about Nick Zicarelli, but she wouldn't confirm any connection between Arnold and her grandpa. Anything I asked along that line, she would reply with something like, 'I don't think that's germane.'"

"Did she give you anything at all to go on?"

"She said Arnold had just about saved enough to attend the school in North Carolina. Which was good because he had just lost his second job."

I had an "aha" moment. "That must have been what prompted the draft letter in his computer."

One hand went to her face as if brushing away the shadows.

"And if he had been working for grandpa, that could have caused the complications he mentioned in the letter to his mom."

I nodded. "Sometimes two and two do add up to four. I think it's time to put on a full-court press. Let me call somebody to patch our driveway, then we'll see if we can pry some answers out of Miss Nikki."

WE DROVE OUT to Green Hills, parked beside the Miata, and rang the doorbell. A startled Nikki Columbo, dressed in jeans and a red sweater emblazoned with prancing reindeer, opened the door and greeted us with wide eyes.

"Has something happened?"

"That's what we came to find out," I said. "May we come in?"

She hesitated a moment but stepped aside and invited us in. The small apartment looked as orderly as a rank of soldiers on parade. The living room was flanked by a bar-like counter that separated it from the kitchen. Gleaming white cabinets matched the appliances. A mauve-colored sectional sofa arranged in a U-shape faced a large-screen TV, an audio deck placed to the side.

Nikki pushed the long black hair over her shoulder and motioned toward the sofa. "Please sit down and tell me what this is all about."

After we were seated, I gave her a solemn look. "I know this past week has been very difficult for you. We don't want to make it any worse, but there are some important points we need to clear up. You know we're involved in the investigation of Arnold's murder."

"But you aren't with the police."

"Correct. We're private detectives working in cooperation with the police. When she called earlier, Jill didn't tell you what happened last night. It pushed this case into a serious new dimension for us."

Her eyes shifted to Jill and back to me.

"Somebody tried to blow up our car...with us in it."

"Oh, my God!" Her hand darted to her mouth.

I pulled up my pants leg to show the bandage. "That's all the damage it did to us, but the car caught on fire. It's totaled."

"Do you know who did it?"

"Afraid not. The fire and explosives experts are still looking into it. We have to assume that it has some relation to our investigation of Arnold's murder."

It wasn't all that certain, of course, but she didn't need to know that.

She sat in stunned silence.

"It appears fairly obvious from what you've told us, and what we've learned from other sources, that Arnold was doing some kind of work for your grandfather Zicarelli. What was it?"

I gave her the most penetrating stare I could muster, one that had loosened the resolve of many a suspect during my OSI career.

Her chin quivered. "I...I can't talk about that."

"Do you think he had anything to do with Arnold's death?"

"No...no!" She sounded panicky.

"You want to expose the murderer, don't you?"

Tears began to flow. "I don't know." She lowered her face into her hands and sobbed.

Jill quickly moved to her side, put an arm around her shoulder, and began to comfort her. "A young girl like you shouldn't have to go through this, but some people have no regard for human life. We have to stop them. We're trying to do what's best for you, Nikki. We have to know all the facts so we can help."

Thinking back over what we did know, I quickly put the pieces together as best I could. Arnold was definitely interested in the betting game, and his mother believed the new job somehow involved gambling. After the interview with Freddie Ford, we were almost certain her suspicions had been right on. According to Wes Knight, Nick Zicarelli was still involved in the wagering business in some manner. Nikki had given Jill the impression that Arnold worked for Zicarelli until he left following some sort of disagreement. The letter in his laptop, if it had been intended for Nikki's grandpa, indicated it involved money. Money for gambling debts he was to collect?

When Nikki stopped crying, I leaned forward and kept my voice soft but firm. "We owe it to Arnold to find out who did this to him. And to you. I think you're trying to protect your grandpa from something that involves Arnold, but not his murder. That's fine. But the police aren't far behind us. If they think Nick Zicarelli might have information relevant to this, they'll pounce on him with both feet. And they won't be gentle about it."

"If you talk to us, we might be able to make things easier," Jill said.

She looked at Jill, then at me, breathing heavily. "I won't do anything to hurt my Grandpa."

"We don't want you to," I said. "All we want to know is why Arnold asked me to meet him at that repair shop last Monday night. What could he have told me that would make a big difference in the effort to bring a pro basketball team to Nashville?"

She stared at me, a puzzled look on her face. "I have no idea."

"What did he tell you after your grandpa let him go?"

"How did—?"

"How did we know about the firing? The police found a

letter on Arnold's computer." I was treading on dangerous ground, discussing confidential police information. I saw it as the only way to shock her into giving us what we were after. "He said he thought he'd been treated unfairly. He thought he'd done as instructed. It wasn't his fault he didn't get the money."

Nikki sat with her mouth open for a moment. "But you said the police didn't know—"

"The police don't know the letter was intended for your grandpa. What did Arnold tell you about it?"

She finally let go. "He was really mad. He said he knew a way to get even, but I told him to calm down and get his temper under control. My Grandpa is an old man, and he can act pretty cranky at times. I intended to talk to him about Arnold."

"What was Arnold's reaction to that?"

"I wasn't too gentle. He apologized, said he hoped he hadn't offended me."

"Was Arnold collecting money for your grandpa?"

That brought a shift in her eyes and a guarded look. "I don't know. I don't think he wanted me to know what he was doing."

She didn't want to hurt her grandfather, so she wasn't willing to say anything that might implicate him in something illegal, like gambling. Arnold was a big enough guy to present a fearsome presence if he chose to. He would have made a dandy debt collector for Nick Zicarelli. Could that figure into the reason behind his murder?

25

ON THE WAY back to the office, Jill complimented me on the manner in which I had handled Nikki's interrogation.

I gave her a dismissive wave. "I can be gentle when the occasion demands."

"A cuddly bear instead of a grizzly?" I could hear the smirk in her voice.

"Let's not get carried away."

"Did Nikki tell you what you wanted to hear?"

"Not all of it," I said. "I'd still like to know exactly what Arnold did for Zicarelli. It sounds like he may have been a bagman. Did he put pressure on people to pay up, or was he just a carrier?"

"Does it matter?"

"It might, if it had something to do with his murder."

"Do you think Nikki's grandpa bears any responsibility for Arnold's death?"

"I'd like to believe he doesn't."

"But you're not sure."

"Right."

"I wonder what Arnold meant by saying he knew how to get even with Zicarelli?"

I reached over and patted her on the knee. "You're a good listener, babe. I've been pondering that same point. Could it be what he was planning to tell me the night he was killed?"

If it was, we'd probably never know, because Arnold was

the only one who could tell us. Unless he had told someone else. But who?

When we got back to the office, I had two calls awaiting me. One from Phil Adamson, the other from Terry Tremont. I reached Phil at his office downtown in the Criminal Justice Center.

"How come you aren't out pounding the pavement looking for bad guys?" I asked.

"The bad guys are all busy doing their Christmas shoplifting. I had a bunch of loose ends and decided this was a good time to look for ways to tie them together. Frankly, I'd rather be home watching some good holiday basketball tournaments."

We'd never talked about playing basketball, but Phil certainly had the height for it. "Now you're getting into my territory," I said. "What do you hear about the NBA recruitment project?"

"I'm not into the pros. College hoops are my passion. The reason I called is I just got the results from those papers Detective Bledsoe salvaged at the library."

"Were they able to decipher anything?"

"Most of it didn't make sense, but there were a couple of interesting things."

"Like 'get Colonel McKenzie'?"

"No, your name wasn't mentioned."

"How about ammonium nitrate and fuel oil?"

"Negative."

"Then what was so interesting?"

"There were indications that Isabell is staying with a Nat Edge in East Nashville. Narcotics says Edge is a known addict and probably does some small-time dealing."

"Where does he live?"

"Sheridan Drive."

That had a familiar ring to it, but I was concentrating too intently on Isabell to catch the connection.

"What's going on with your case?" he asked.

I looked around at Jill, who busily scrolled down the page in her computer, looking as frustrated as I felt. "Using a basketball analogy, it's half-time and we're down fifty to thirty. Got any good pep talks we could use?"

Phil laughed. "Sounds like the score in most of my cases. I could use a few free throws for sure."

"Remember the girl named Columbo I told you about? Turns out she wasn't much help, but I learned she's a granddaughter of Nick Zicarelli. What can you tell me about him?"

"Nick's an old-time gambler. Ran a roadhouse operation on the north side years ago."

"Yeah, I heard about that. Anything in recent times?"

"I never had any dealings with him. I've heard vice guys talk about him, though. They say he only indulges in big-money betting, so they figure no little guys are gettiong fleeced. They decided he wasn't worth spending a lot of resources on. If you caught him, it would probably involve some big shot around town who would put pressure on the mayor or the chief. That could lead to a lot of bad press. You know how cops shy away from all that notoriety."

"Cops are shy?" I chuckled. "All the smiling badges I've seen on the tube lately, you could've fooled me."

"Don't get me started on that. I've told you what I think of those self-aggrandizing types who think they have to take a bow every time they stop a DUI."

"Yeah, reminds me of Detective Tremaine, when he was riding high in the saddle." I couldn't forget my old nemesis and his handling of the Tessa Peterson disappearance two years ago that got me in trouble with the DA. "He relished every minute he stood in front of a camera. Funny, I don't see much of him anymore."

"He got his wings clipped."

"How'd that happen?"

"It was sort of a replay of the Peterson case. Tremaine spent days chasing after a guy when the guilty party was practically parked under his nose."

"Nice to hear," I said, feeling more vindicated. "What else can you tell me about Zicarelli?"

Phil muttered for a moment, then said, "Okay, just remember you didn't hear this from me. You need a little background on the Nashville criminal element that you won't find in any police report. I don't mean the petty thieves and drug runners. I'm talking about the big boys.

"Some years back, four guys involved in local organized crime split up the city into geographical zones. Nick was one of them. He had closed his club, but he owned another restaurant closer in. He stocked it with illegal gambling machines. He also arranged to put them in other places around his zone."

"Didn't he get raided?"

"Sure. But he had a son who was a cop. Nick always got tipped off before a raid. He had a crew that would go around and pick up the machines and haul them off to his warehouse. They would leave a few around to be found and keep everybody happy. Nick supported all the politicians' favorite causes, sponsored an annual picnic for officeholders. He was the all-around good guy with a hand in everybody's pocket. He made tons of money. When he got into his late sixties, he turned the day-to-day business over to another son and retired to handling only big bettors. He's almost untouchable."

Jill was on the other line when I finished with Phil, so I called our client.

"I suppose you saw that little note in the morning paper about us," I said when Terry came on the line.

"Yeah. Your car blew up in the driveway. What the devil is going on? What does 'unknown origin' mean?"

"It means we don't know who the hell did it." I caught Jill's frown but only shrugged. I believe my wife could pick up a cuss word from a block away in a thunderstorm. But the thought of my Jeep's fate and my inability to pinpoint the culprit was getting to me.

"The story said no one was seriously injured." Terry's voice held a note of sympathy.

"Right. I got a cut on my leg that required a few stitches. I'll live."

"Was there any indication it involved our case?" Terry asked.

"Not directly, but I have to assume that's quite likely what it was. Of course, there's one other possibility."

I told him about the former navigator I had helped send to prison, who was out now and apparently looking for revenge. As I thought about it, I realized where I had run into Sheridan Drive before.

"The cops found Izzy Isabell at a house on Sheridan Drive in East Nasville," I said. "That's the street where Jill was held two years ago after that Palestinian group abducted her. Isabell's staying at the home of a guy named Nat Edge, a drug addict."

"Sounds like Izzy might be your bomber," Terry said.

"I'm reserving judgment. I hope he learned his lesson. He got a tougher sentence because he tried to recruit somebody to murder prosecution witnesses. Scratching up my car sounds like he's more of a threat to make himself a nuisance now. The cops are keeping an eye on him."

"If the bombing was related to our case, it surely means

you're getting a bit too close for somebody's comfort."

"I'd like to think so."

I also told him about Nikki Columbo's grandfather, Nick Zicarelli, and what Sam Gannon had heard regarding a little discord in the ranks of the basketball crowd.

"Brad Smotherman will be happy to hear things aren't going smoothly," Terry said. "As for old Nick Z, I'm familiar with him. The high school where he played has a trophy named for him. They say he was quite a player in his day. I'm sure he'd be happy if Nashville got a pro team. I understand he's a familiar figure at the NBA playoffs. Knowing his reputation, I suspect he has a big finger in the betting pie, too."

"We don't know that he has any role in this NBA deal, or in Arnold Wechsel's murder, but we're digging hard to find out."

"After what happened last night, it sounds like you two had better be careful and watch your flanks," Terry said.

I intended to. I planned to move carefully as I sought answers to the puzzle Arnold Wechsel had left behind, but I was determined to find what he knew that would blow my mind. I still felt a twinge of guilt that he was murdered on my watch.

When I got off the phone, I turned to tell Jill what I'd learned from Phil and Terry. She beat me to the draw.

"I hope you were careful in what you said to Phil. We led Nikki to believe we'd go easier on her grandpa than the police would. If you give Phil a reason to go after Zicarelli, Nikki will find out about it and we can write her off as a source."

"I was circumspect," I said.

"What did Phil say about him?"

I related the story of Zicarelli's gambling background and his current posture. "He may not admit anything to us," I said, "but I think it would be worth a trip out to push him a bit."

She gave me a skeptical look. "From what Phil told you, it doesn't sound like he'd be an easy one to push."

I grinned. "You know my motto, babe. The bigger they come, the harder they fall." It was mostly bravado to keep her from worrying too much. I knew the chances were slim, but that had never stopped me from trying.

I checked his address and found he lived in Whites Creek, a small community on the north side of town with its own post office but not much else. It wasn't too far from where his long-defunct Sporting Executives Club had been located. Whites Creek's most notable feature was Fontanel, the 27,000-square-foot mansion built by country music superstar Barbara Mandrell in 1988. Despite what Phil had told me, I suspected Zicarelli's abode would be a bit more modest.

We ate a quick lunch at the restaurant across the center and headed out Old Hickory Boulevard. The circumferential highway took us around the eastern edge of the county, then west through Madison and across two interstates. The road wound about an area of farms with fallow fields and leafless woodlands, spiced up by an occasional large home. We turned left at Whites Creek Pike. This intersection housed another of the community's notable features, Richard's Louisiana Café, which advertised "live music, dead crawfish." We had once visited Richard's with a client who loved Cajun-style food.

Houses were few and far between along here. We cruised slowly until we spotted a mailbox with Zicarelli's address in front of a large two-story house that sat at least a hundred yards off the road. The afternoon sun glistened off its pristine coat of white paint. With four tall columns in front, it resembled Andrew Jackson's Hermitage, which I suspected was the catalyst for the architect's design.

We headed up the paved driveway and pulled into a circular parking area beside a Lincoln Town Car. We walked up to the broad front porch with its double-door entrance, and I rang the bell. After a few moments, we found ourselves facing a tall, slender man with bushy white hair and eyebrows and a set to his mouth that made me think stubborn. I figured it was indicative of Nikki's characterization of her grandfather as "cranky at times."

"Mr. Zicarelli?" I asked.

"That's me," he said. "Who are you?"

"Greg and Jill McKenzie." I handed him a business card. "We're private investigators."

He glanced at the card and handed it back. "I don't need any investigating, thank you very much."

"We're looking into the murder of Arnold Wechsel," I said.

"I don't know anything about that."

"It's a bit cold out here, Mr. Zicarelli," Jill said. "Could we come in and talk to you for a few minutes?"

He obviously wasn't thrilled with the idea, but I figured he was too much of a gentleman to refuse her. He pulled open the door and stood aside. We entered a large wood-floored foyer with a circular staircase in back. He directed us to a large parlor off to the right. Furnished in pale colors with oversize pieces of furniture, it possessed the formal look of one of those rooms people normally ignore in favor of more casual digs.

"I don't know anything about a murder," he said when we were seated. "I didn't read the story."

"But you knew there was a story about Arnold's murder?" I asked, rumpling my brow.

He just stared, his jaw set.

"What was Arnold Wechsel doing for you?" I asked.

"Who said I knew Arnold Wechsel?"

"Your granddaughter."

His nostrils flared. "You stay away from my granddaughter."

"She was very circumspect in what she told us. She wouldn't say anything she thought might be harmful to you. But she admitted that Arnold worked for you, and that you let him go."

"That boy talked too much," Zicarelli said with a scowl.

I found that accusation astonishing. Our experience, and that of everyone else we had talked to, indicated he was a very close-mouthed young man. Perhaps Zicarelli meant Arnold had talked too much to Nikki. I didn't want to cause her any trouble, but I was determined to squeeze something out of her grandpa.

"Was Arnold collecting money for you?" I asked.

"What Arnold Wechsel or anybody else did for me is none of your damned business."

"Was it gambling debts?"

He jumped up and jammed his fists against his hips, surprisingly agile for someone his size and age. "To hell with you! I don't have to answer any of this nonsense. I have a son who's been a policeman for years. Only cops are authorized to investigate murders."

I stood facing him. "For your information, Mr. Zicarelli, Arnold called me Monday afternoon and said he had some information for me. He asked me to meet him that night at an auto repair shop off Dickerson Road. I'm the one who found his body."

His arms dropped to his sides. His eyes narrowed and the bushy brows merged.

I wanted to put pressure on him by mentioning Homicide Detective Phil Adamson, but I decided I'd pushed my luck far enough with Nikki. "Do you have any idea what Arnold planned to tell me Monday night?"

"Hell, no!"

His reply came as sharp as the crack of a rifle.

"Thank you, Mr. Zicarelli," I said, motioning to Jill. "Let's go. I think our business here is finished."

I knew we'd have as much chance of getting answers from a bronze statue as we would Nick Zicarelli. I didn't look back as we walked toward the foyer, but I heard no movement behind us. I held the front door open for Jill, then followed her out.

26

WHEN I CLIMBED into the car and looked around at Jill, I saw an apprehensive frown. "Knowing what we know about Nick Zicarelli," she said, "it sounds like he would make a formidable enemy. Doesn't that worry you?"

"True, from his reactions, I don't think he considers me a good pal. But danger?" I shrugged. "I was happy to see that Lincoln beside us instead of a Cadillac."

She opened her purse and palmed the snub-nosed .38. "I kept this handy while you talked to him."

She handled the gun with total familiarity, though for years she'd been highly critical of firearms and the necessity for my carrying one. How times changed. "I didn't feel threatened," I said, "but I didn't feel it wise to push any harder, either."

"You know we're going to have to confide in Phil at some point."

I nodded in agreement. "And soon."

I pulled out of the driveway glancing up at a bank of dark-tinged, ribbed clouds that had moved in while we were in Whites Creek. It left the landscape a mottled gray. Though the digital clock on the dash showed it was only mid-afternoon, headlights along Old Hickory Boulevard made it seem that twilight lurked just around the corner.

"Are those snow clouds?" I asked.

Jill, the pilot and family meteorologist, turned on her teacher voice. "Low stratiform clouds can mean either rain or snow. Whether we get any kind of precipitation depends on the temperature and dew point. I don't think the forecasters are predicting anything but clouds."

"Maybe the weather folks are saving up for a white Christmas."

"That'll be the day."

I knew what she meant. Since moving to Jill's hometown, I'd learned there were a lot more reliable reasons for coming to Nashville then wanting to experience a white Christmas. That wasn't a problem for me, though. I enjoyed Christmas however it came, and right now it was coming in the midst of a perplexing case that mixed murder with mischief, including the possibility of an NBA basketball scandal. I was more convinced than ever that Arnold Wechsel's death had a direct tie to our investigation. I suspected Nick Zicarelli could shed a great deal more light on the subject than he was willing to provide.

Before we made it back to Hermitage, Jill's cell phone serenaded us with a snippet from The Nutcracker Suite. After answering, she looked a bit startled and said, "Well, hello, Mr. Aregis."

I gave her a curious glance. What the devil could he be calling about?

She listened a few moments, then said, "Hold on a minute, let me check something on my calendar."

She muted the phone and turned to me. "He wants to discuss something, said we could meet at a lounge at five. What should I do?"

I didn't like the idea. On the other hand, it undoubtedly involved the NBA deal. It could be an opportunity to learn something that might bolster our case. At this point, we badly needed bolstering.

I made a snap decision, something I normally avoid.

"Okay, but make sure it's at a reputable place where I can lurk in the shadows."

She squinched her eyes nearly shut and shook her head. "I can make it," she said into the phone. "Where would you like to meet?"

She flipped the phone shut a moment later, and I asked, "Where?"

"The Black Watch. It's a lounge on West End, out past Vanderbilt. I thought you'd approve of that."

The Black Watch, known as the Royal Regiment of Scotland, was one of the most celebrated fighting units in the world. Jill and I had attended a performance of the Black Watch Pipes and Drums at the Performing Arts Center a couple of years back. I'd never been to the lounge and suspected its name was the only thing Scottish about it, but the location wasn't bad.

"You realize Nick Zicarelli could have called Aregis and told him about our visit," I said.

"In the first place, we have no proof that Zicarelli even knows Aregis. And in the second place, there's no way Aregis could have connected the name Jill Parsons to McKenzie Investigations."

"Okay," I said. "Why don't we use this opportunity to put some of our spycraft to work?"

"You mean those surveillance gadgets you picked up the other day at the Covert Security store?"

"Right. We'll fix you up with a concealed microphone and transmitter. I'll sit at a table across the room with the receiver unit. I'll record the conversation and listen live with an earpiece. I don't expect any problems, but should anything happen, I'll be right there."

I saw a twinkle in her eye that usually meant trouble. "Are you sure we need to use all this spy stuff?" she asked. "Or is it a case of not trusting your little wife with another man?"

I made a face. "I trust my little wife but not the other man."

When we got to the office, the answering machine held a call from a sobbing Nikki Columbo.

"Grandpa hates me," she said in a barely decipherable moan.

I looked at Jill. "I think you'd better handle this one."

She gave a deep sigh. "I should make you take it. You set her up with what you said to her grandpa."

Jill made the call, however, and I picked up my extension to listen in. Nikki was still sniffling when she answered.

"Just calm down, Nikki, and get your wits about you," Jill said. "Your grandpa doesn't hate you. Remember, you told us he can be pretty cranky at times."

"He was really angry because I talked to you."

"I suspect he was more upset because we talked to him."

"But he said it was my fault."

"You need to explain to him that we're only interested in finding out who killed Arnold and why."

"Grandpa believes you think he had something to do with it."

"I don't remember us saying anything to give him that idea."

"He thinks I told you that Arnold was collecting money for him."

She hadn't, but that pretty well confirmed for me that it was precisely what Arnold had been doing.

"Greg told him that you were very circumspect in what you said to us. When your grandpa cools down, I'm sure he'll feel bad about what he said to you. Don't worry about it, dear. You'll be okay."

Before Jill finished, the other line rang. It was Brad Smotherman.

"Can you make it to the Pred's hockey game tonight?" he asked. "We're playing the Anaheim Ducks. Mack Nelson will be there. It'll give you a chance to talk to him. You can join us in the Hatrick Suite."

The young country music star was the last principal in the case for us to interview, and I had an important question for him. After Jill's date for cocktails, we could have dinner and then join Smotherman at the game.

"Sure," I said, "we'll see you at the arena."

A green-suited delivery woman walked in a few minutes later with a colorfully-wrapped gift, a red bow on top. Her dark hair tied in a ponytail, she swung her head around to check the tag on the package.

"Looking for Lieutenant Colonel Greg McKenzie," she said.

I grinned. "That's me."

"Sounds like you'll be having a liquid Christmas," she said, shaking the box gently.

I took the package, thanked her, and signed for it. Jill came over to see what I had. I pulled the card off and read:

"Merry Christmas from your old friends in the OSI. Congratulations on the great job you're doing in your new career."

"I wonder who thought of that?" Jill asked.

Good question.

I tore off the wrapping and opened a gift box containing a fancy glass decanter of Scotch. It wasn't my preferred brand, but it was a good one. "Not a bad choice," I said.

"Could it be from Jeff Price?"

"I think Jeff would've signed his name to it."

"What about Colonel Grigsby?"

I tilted the bottle and took a closer look. "That's more likely. He's the only one I've had contact with lately."

"And it's the sort of thing he would do," Jill said.

"Since you're going out for cocktails, I might as well sample it."

"But I'll be on official business." She pointed at the Scotch. "That's pure pleasure."

"At least we agree on that." I smiled. "This isn't your drink of choice, but you can at least have a sip. We'll toast the coming solution to this case."

I tore the tax stamp that sealed the container while she brought over a couple of small glasses. Twisting off the crystal top, I poured a small amount for each of us.

I handed one to Jill, raised my glass, and said, "Here's to nailing the killer."

As I lowered the drink, I got a whiff of the aroma. An alarm went off in my head. It carried the jolt of a fire bell.

Jill had her glass almost to her lips.

"Don't drink that!" I yelled.

Startled, she nearly spilled it.

I shouted out the words. "It's cyanide. I know that bitter almond smell. I was exposed to it once at a forensic lab."

27

JILL STARED AT the drink in her hand. "It's in the whisky?"

"Right." I checked the torn tax stamp that sealed the bottle. It wouldn't pull away with a gentle tug. In my experience, those things weren't stuck on that securely. The loose end wouldn't budge. Looking at it more closely, I saw what appeared to be glue residue around the edges.

"It looks like this stamp has been pulled off and glued back on," I said. "Somebody has tampered with this."

I called Phil Adamson's cell phone and found him at a service station in Donelson, which was the next exit down I-40 from our office. He said he would drop by in fifteen or twenty minutes.

"Could it have been Izzy Isabell?" Jill asked.

"If so, we're in a lot more trouble than I thought."

When Phil arrived, I showed him the carafe and explained my suspicions.

He examined the whisky bottle carefully without touching it. "I see your point about the stamp," he said. "And you think you smelled cyanide? Not everybody can detect that stuff, you know."

"I can. I got a whiff of it at a lab once."

"Do you think it might be the work of your old navigator?"

"That's what Jill asked. It's certainly possible."

"I'll get it checked out, but you know how long it takes to get toxicology results."

"Since we have reason to suspect cyanide, can't they do a quick test to see if it's present?"

"I should think so."

I took a pencil and propped up the card with its innocuous greeting. "This looks a little sophisticated for Isabell. Maybe he learned some new tricks in prison."

"I'll have everything checked for fingerprints, then send it for a tox report," Phil said. "You going to question whoever delivered it?"

"Yeah. I'll give them a call. I'd like to go over there, but Jill and I are running a little operation out West End at five o'clock, then we're meeting with a client at the Pred's game."

Phil looked back at the Scotch. "If this is from Isabell, at least we know where to find him."

After he left, I called the delivery company and explained the problem. I asked where the package had originated.

"Right here," the man said after checking his records. "It was brought in this morning by a Victor Lewis."

"Do you have an address?"

"It's 1830 Sheridan Drive. Zip is 37206."

That settled it as far as I was concerned. I'd bet there was no Victor Lewis on Sheridan Drive, probably not even an 1830. This was the work of Izzy Isabell. I turned to my computer and did a quick search. I was right on both counts. Sheridan addresses started with 1900.

I turned to Jill. "The person who sent the Scotch gave a fake name and address. The fictitious address was on Sheridan Drive."

"If it was Isabell, do you think he'll try something else now?" Her face mirrored her concern.

"Not until he finds this didn't work. Hopefully the cops will have the evidence to go after him by then." It was by no means a certainty. First they had to confirm the Scotch contained a poison, then they'd have to identify who sent it. I needed to check the delivery company in the morning and get a description of the man who claimed to be Victor Lewis.

WE CLOSED SHOP around four and went home. After getting Jill wired with the microphone and transmitter, I checked the equipment to make sure everything worked as advertised. We headed for I-40 just in time to keep her from being late for her date.

The Black Watch sat beside a building with shops on the first two floors, parking above. I pulled into the garage so Aregis wouldn't see Jill getting out of the Camry. We switched on the electronic equipment before starting for the lounge. Workers from nearby offices whose day ended at four-thirty bustled along the sidewalk with collars turned up against the cold. I followed Jill at a safe distance, listening through my earpiece receiver that resembled a Bluetooth telephone gadget. I felt sure any curious onlookers would take it for that.

Before I entered the place, I picked up Jill's voice talking to someone I assumed to be Louie Aregis. Inside, a busty blonde with a come-hither smile greeted me and steered me across the room from the table occupied by my wife and the Coastal Capital owner. I took a chair against the wall facing them. I didn't need to worry about being recognized, even if Aregis had seen me before. The lighting in the Black Watch was so dim you'd hardly know your neighbor.

The lounge had a compact bar at one side and a slightly-raised stage in the back, where I saw a drum set and a few guitars leaning on stands. A large replica of the distinctive Black Watch military badge was mounted on the wall. One small spotlight overhead provided more illumination than I could detect anywhere else but over the bar. A mixture of business types, dressed in everything from Brooks Brothers to

Men's Wearhouse, and well-coifed young women I assumed had just come from work occupied most of the tables. When the waitress came around, I ordered a Scotch and soda. Being true to my roots, I asked for Glenfiddich, the only Highland single malt distilled, aged, and bottled at the distillery. Happily, they had it.

As my little earpiece blared with the conversation across the room, Aregis did most of the talking. At first it was "nice to see you again" and "how have you been?" When they ordered, I suspected he was trying to impress Jill that he was now a true Tennessean. He asked for Jack Daniel's and water. Jill chose her favorite wine, Zinfandel.

"My secretary looked around at a few newsstands but couldn't find your magazine," he said after a few minutes. "When will the article be published?"

Uh oh, I thought. I hoped the lady hadn't asked the store if they could order a copy. She would have been told that *Sporting World* was not among magazines listed in their computer.

Jill didn't hesitate. "The editors work several weeks ahead. It'll be a while before that issue comes out. I'll be happy to let you know when it does."

That seemed to satisfy him, but he promptly hit on another touchy subject. "I see by your rings that you're married. What does your husband do?"

My wife is about as moral a person as I've ever met. I had a real problem convincing her that in detective work it was necessary to masquerade your motives occasionally. I told her it wasn't the same as ordinary lying. It was more like a solder's camouflage, changing appearances to protect yourself or your operation. She finally bought into it but now used her wiles to stick with the truth. "He's retired military," she said. "Air Force."

"Was he a pilot?"

"No, he was an investigator."

"Interesting."

Before he could push the question further, she outflanked him. "The name Aregis is rather unusual. I found a reference to it as being Greek. Is that where your parents came from?"

"Actually, my father came from Greece. An area near the Turkish border. My mother was from a small town in Sicily. So I guess I'm Greco-Italian."

That mention of Sicily rang a bell. I recalled Vernon Quillen mentioning talk that Aregis' mother's family had Mafia connections.

"Did your parents settle in Florida when they came to the United States?" Jill asked.

"Yes, but they didn't come over together. They met in Miami and were married there, before moving to Orlando, where I was born. My mother had relatives in Miami, but Dad was the only Aregis to immigrate."

"Do you have any brothers or sisters?"

"No, I was an only child."

"So was I. My father sold insurance for one of the major companies, and my mother played classical violin. She was in the Nashville Symphony during my younger days."

"I haven't had a chance to attend a symphony concert here. We were symphony patrons in Pensacola, but I've been too busy with the move and getting the business re-established in Nashville."

I could make out Jill resting her elbows on the table and folding her hands, although it was difficult to tell much of what was going on in that cave-like atmosphere. "Does your wife like classical music?" she asked. "You said she was a country music fan."

"Uh...oh, yes. She likes all kinds of music. It's just that country is her favorite."

What a jerk. That lame excuse was made up on the spur of the moment to help justify the move.

"Have there been any new developments in the NBA franchise affair since we talked?" she asked.

"That's really why I wanted you to meet me here. As you probably know, the local news outlets aren't too kind to so-called 'outsiders.' I'm supposed to be the chief spokesman for this deal, but they defer to Howard Hays, who's a local legend. Writing for a national publication, you have a wider perspective. I'm sure you have media contacts here."

"Yes," Jill said. "At the newspaper and one of the TV stations in particular."

I sipped sparingly on my drink and grinned. She referred to my reporter buddy, Wes Knight, and our new Channel 4 contact, Rod Jenson.

"Howard is a conservative who wants to keep everything under wraps until we have a firm deal. We need to stir up the public and get them behind this thing. I want to get the word out that Coastal Capital Ventures is committed one hundred percent to bringing this city a National Basketball Association team. I want the people to push the City Council for unanimous support of our efforts."

Good luck, I thought. With five at large seats and thirty-five representing districts, you'd have a real problem getting the Metro Council to unanimously agree on the time of day.

"I'll let you in on a little secret," he said. "But you have to agree to keep it confidential until it's been cleared. Agreed?"

"My lips are sealed."

I had to grin at that, too. "My" was the operative word. She made no promises as to what her husband might do.

"We've begun some serious discussions with an owner," he said. "I can't tell you who, but it's a start. I'm hopeful it won't take long to get a workable deal."

"That's great news," Jill said. "I'm sure Mr. Hays and Mr. Ricketts are elated about that."

"They're pretty naïve at this sort of thing. Frankly, they'd be lost without me."

That got him started on a long, pompous oration about all the high-powered dealing he had done. After listening a bit, I checked my watch and decided we'd heard enough of Nashville's new savior from the Promised Land to the south. I took out my cell phone and speed-dialed Jill. I heard her phone ring.

"Hello."

"It's time to wrap this up, babe," I said. "We need to get something to eat before we head to the hockey game. Tell Mr. Wonderful good night."

"Okay," she said. "I'll be along in a few minutes."

I heard her tell him she had to wrap it up. I signaled the waitress to pay my check. When Aregis offered to escort Jill to her car, she said that wouldn't be necessary as she needed to stop at a store in the building next door. I walked out ahead of her, then moseyed along until I heard her say good-bye. I glanced around and saw her come out of the Black Watch Lounge alone.

We rendezvoused in the building's elevator lobby.

"What did you think of Prince Charming?" she asked with a mischievous grin.

I shook my head. "There's not much doubt about what he thinks of himself."

"He has a lot of charisma, if you can take the narcissism."

"Unfortunately, they often go hand in hand. But I'm afraid our client isn't going to feel charmed when he hears the news about their discussions with an NBA owner."

28

WE ARRIVED EARLY at the arena, located downtown at Fifth Avenue and Broadway. The first of Nashville's hotly-disputed, big-ticket, publicly-funded sports projects, and the smallest at only $150 million, the arena was fronted by a twenty-two-story tower that squeezed down to what looked like a radio station antenna. The arena itself, viewed at night from high up in a downtown hotel, resembled a clamshell opening with bared teeth, if clams had teeth. We picked up the tickets Smotherman had left for us and took an elevator to the Suite Level.

With the distinctive Hatrick Brake Company logo at the door, we had no trouble finding the correct location. Inside, it featured a counter with a variety of snack foods, a large flat-panel TV screen above, and another table with a roll top food warmer. A row of chairs behind a serving counter faced the ice rink, with two rows of seats beyond, angled down toward the ice. A small Christmas tree covered with colorful lights and ornaments stood in one corner of the room. A green wreath and garlands of red and silver decked the walls.

"Glad you could make it," a beaming Brad Smotherman said as he hurried over to welcome us. He wore similar casual garb to what we'd seen at his office.

"We take in a game now and then," I said, "but we've never been to the suites before. Nice location."

"We're almost on the red line, and we're high enough to get an excellent view of the ice."

The red line was hockey's equivalent of football's fifty-yard line. I gazed out over the expanse of white below. Although this was more like a working vacation, I gave the work part top priority. "When will Mack Nelson be here?"

"Just talked to him. He's on the way. Gordon said he'd drop by, also. He's in a different suite. Sample the food and make yourselves at home. There's a restroom over there if you need to use it. I think that's where my wife is now."

He introduced us to a couple of visiting automaker execs and one of his top company staffers who would be watching the game with us. One of the Detroit types talked about how he enjoyed getting away from all the snow, although the frosty air made him feel like he was back home. Moments later an attractive Asian woman came out of the restroom and headed toward us.

"Maruko," said Smotherman, "meet the McKenzies, Greg and Jill. My wife, Maruko."

She shook my hand and then Jill's. "You're the ones working with Terry Tremont. So nice to meet you. I'm happy you were able to be with us tonight."

She had dark hair that nearly covered her forehead and fell short on the sides. Dressed in a white shirt with the Predator's sabretooth tiger logo, she had a pretty face that showed few hints of being as old as her husband. I'd always marveled at how some Japanese women did such a great job of masking their true age.

"We're looking forward to the game," Jill said. "Hopefully we'll also come up with some ideas that will make it worthwhile from Terry's standpoint."

"I'm sure that would make him happy," I said. "Incidentally, the Christmas décor looks great. I suspect that's your doings, Mrs. Smotherman."

"Please, call me Maruko. And you're a good detective, Greg.

The treee and garlands were, indeed, my idea. I love this season."

I told Brad about the latest developments in our investigation, including our suspicions regarding Nick Zicarelli's connection to Arnold Wechsel. When I related what Louie Aregis had told Jill about their negotiations with an NBA owner, he pounded his fist against the countertop.

"Crap! We need to crank up our efforts. We need proof that something off-color is going on with these guys."

Jill darted an anxious look my way, but before I could reply, everyone's attention shifted to the suite entrance. The door opened and three chattering young men made their entry as noisy as a flock of pigeons. I recognized Mack Nelson in his dust-brown cowboy hat, jeans, and square-toed boots. A lean, wiry young man, he looked rugged enough to have come off a ranch. But I knew he hadn't. He grew up on the south side of Memphis, the son of a pizza shop manager. A shorter man, a little older, also wore a cowboy hat. The trailing figure appeared middle thirties, hard as a cedar post, with dark, searching eyes. A security type if I'd ever seen one.

"Hi, everybody," Nelson greeted us.

Smotherman patted him on the shoulder and shook his hand. "Come in, Mack. Meet our guests, Greg and Jill McKenzie. I told you they needed to have a few words. I thought we could get that done before the game starts."

Mack shook hands and nodded to Maruko.

"I appreciate your coming," I said. "We've already talked to your two Protect Our Preds partners, and we need to touch bases with you. I'm sure you know about the murder of a young guy named Arnold Wechsel last Saturday. We think it's tied in with this NBA deal, and we're trying to track down the connection."

Mack Nelson nodded. "I haven't had much time to read

the local papers, but Brad told me about what's been goin' on."
He looked around and motioned to the man in the cowboy hat.
"This is Deke Bragg, folks. He's my band leader. He keeps me
on key and all that good stuff. The fella over there against the
wall givin' y'all the evil eye is Rocky Topp. Swears that's his
real name, but I dunno. Anyway, he's paid to see I don't wind
up like that Wechsel boy."

After a quick trip to the snack bar, Brad, Mack, Jill, and I
pulled chairs together next to the wall. I gave Mack a brief
summary of what we had uncovered so far, adding a bit about
the explosion in our driveway the night before.

His hazel eyes widened. "They blew up your car?"

"That's right. We have no proof that somebody associated
with this case did it, but that seems the most likely explanation."

"Dang. Maybe I'd better lend you my man Rocky."

"The best thing you can do is think hard about anything
you know that might help us pin down what's going on here.
Brad tells us you were the one who picked up the rumor that
something wasn't right about the NBA situation."

He crossed his legs and wiggled the boot from side to side.
"Actually, it came from a member of the band. I promised I'd
leave his name out of it."

"Exactly what did he hear?" I asked.

"He's got a Porsche Carrera GT that his brother bought
just before he died. It's a high performance car that he gets
serviced at a race car shop. Seems he was over there last week
and overheard a mechanic talkin' on the phone. He sounded
real put out. He was sayin' something like 'I can ruin that
basketball deal if I tell what that man's done.'"

Jill and I glanced at each other. It had to have been Arnold
Wechsel.

"Did he say what the mechanic looked like?" I asked.

"No. Just told me what he heard."

"I need to talk to him," I said. "This could be the break we're looking for."

Mack narrowed his eyes and twisted his mouth. "He doesn't want to get involved, and I promised I wouldn't use his name."

"After what Louie Aregis told them tonight, this could really be important, Mack," Smotherman said. "That musician has to talk to Greg."

"Why don't you ask him to call us," Jill said. "We don't care about his name. We only need to know exactly what he heard, and who he heard it from."

Mack folded his arms and looked around. "Okay, I'll give it a try."

"Do more than try, son," Smotherman said. "See that he calls Greg."

The hockey game started a few minutes later, and we watched the action as fans yelled and screamed around us. Ice hockey is the fastest game in sports and the crowd really gets into it. The constant movement tends to keep you on the edge of your seat through all three of its twenty-minute periods. During the first break, while the Zamboni resurfacer cruised about smoothing the ice, Gordon Franklin wandered into the suite.

He talked to Smotherman a moment, then walked over to where Jill and I sat.

"Enjoying the game?" he asked, the hint of a smile on his face. It was about as animated as we'd seen him.

At this point, the Preds were ahead 1-zip.

"It's been pretty exciting," Jill said.

I stood and looked down at him. "Good game so far. Have you had any thoughts about what's been going on with this basketball group?"

"No. I've been out of the office a couple of days. I've had

nothing on my mind but profit and loss statements, cash flow reports, and the like."

"We haven't been so lucky," I said.

He frowned. "What do you mean?"

"You haven't heard about the bomb that destroyed my Jeep?"

His face took on an I'm-not-believing-this look. "Heavens, no."

I gave him the short version of what happened in our driveway.

He rubbed his chin as though stroking a beard. "I'd say you'd better be careful what you're doing."

"We plan to. And I pity the guy who did this when I find him," I said.

"When?"

I smiled. "When."

"Well, good luck," he said before heading over to the food counter.

The Ducks scored in the second period, and the game remained tied until the last minute of play. When the Preds scored on a power play with 20 seconds left, the crowd went wild. Jill and I stood and cheered along with everybody else.

After the clock on the scoreboard flashed double zero, I turned to Brad Smotherman. "Thanks for setting this up. We enjoyed the game, but now we need to get home and wait for that phone call."

"I hope it proves productive," Smotherman said.

He wasn't the only one. After that earlier outburst, I had the feeling we were on a short leash with this case.

THE PHONE RANG just after eleven o'clock.

"Mr. McKenzie?" said a hushed male voice.

"This is he."

"Mack Nelson said I should call you. What is it you want to know?"

"Could you describe the mechanic you overheard talking on the phone?"

"Well, he was a big guy, six feet or more, and young. And he had an accent."

"German?"

"I'd say it was."

"Did he use any names, maybe who he was talking to?"

"I don't think so."

"Can you recall his exact words?"

"I'm not positive, but it was like 'damn him, I can ruin that NBA deal if I tell what he's done.' Then he said 'I'm not sure who to tell, but I'll find out.'"

29

AN ICY WIND moaned in the trees Friday morning. The gas heating unit shifted into overdrive as the mercury hovered in the low 20s. I used a plastic bag to cover my damaged leg before getting into the shower. The steamy water considerably improved my outlook, and Jill had to coax me out with a caution that breakfast would be cold if I didn't hurry. Turned out she had fixed hot oatmeal, which tasted especially good with plenty of butter and brown sugar. The coffee helped, too. I used it to wash down two Texas-sized cinnamon rolls. Oddly, she didn't object to the double dose of pastry this time. I presumed she felt magnanimous because it was Christmas Eve.

"I'm not sure how much we can get done today," Jill said, "since most businesses will be closing early. A lot of them will have Christmas parties. I remember years ago going to some real doozies at my dad's office. Not much work got done."

I reminded her of one pressing matter. "We need to check into who sent that bottle of Scotch yesterday."

Jill looked around from loading the dishwasher. "I wonder if the Fire Marshal's office, or the ATF, or the TBI Lab will be working as usual today?"

"I'll give Jed Clampett a call when we get to the office and see if I he's turned up anything."

"Would this be a good day to look for you a car?"

"Maybe. Let's see how it goes."

I checked the driveway carefully when we left for work. I

wouldn't be surprised at another attempt on our lives by whoever had planted the bomb, but I expected any new effort would come in a different form. That prospect plus Izzy Isabell still running loose out there meant we'd have to remain as vigilant as soldiers on patrol.

I drove straight to the local office of Express Delivery Service, off Elm Hill Pike near the airport. An older man with an abundant white beard that made him resemble a character out of a nursery rhyme greeted us from behind the counter.

I handed him a business card and explained our problem with the package I had received yesterday.

"I need to talk to whoever accepted it," I said. "We're trying to identify the man who brought it in and gave a false identification."

He squinted through his large, round glasses. "Who was the package to?"

"Lieutenant Colonel Greg McKenzie was on the card."

"Yeah, I remember. That was me," he said. "It was a young fellow, not much more'n a teenager. He gave me a piece of paper with your name and address written on it. Paid with a twenty-dollar bill."

"Do you still have the paper with the address on it?"

"No. He wanted it back. Don't know why."

I did. Lieutenant Isabell, if he was the culprit, had probably paid the boy well to bring in the package and retrieve anything that might be used as evidence.

AS SOON AS WE arrived at the office, Jill put on water for cappuccino.

"I'll go up the street and get us some doughnuts," I said. "That'll be our office Christmas Party."

She laughed. "Don't bother, dear. I brought some banana bread from the freezer. It'll be thawed enough for partying."

She had just turned on the computer to check our email when the phone rang. I glanced at the caller ID and saw it was from Germany.

"I'll get it," I said.

When I answered, Jeff Price had a strange tale to relate.

"Arnold's mother got a mystifying call a little while ago that really freaked her out," he said. "It showed Arnold's cell phone number in Nashville, but when she answered, nobody was on the line. She called back and it rang but nobody answered."

Arnold's cell phone. I slapped my forehead with the palm of my hand. Idiot! What was I thinking? Now I knew what had been bugging me the past several days.

"Do you have Arnold's number, Jeff?" I asked.

"No, but I can get it for you."

"Please."

"I'll call you right back."

I switched off the phone and turned to Jill. She stared at me like I had lost my mind, and that's the way I felt.

"Arnold had a cell phone," I said. "Remember, his neighbor said she heard him talking angrily on the phone in the hallway to some guy named Frank."

Jill shook her head. "And neither of us caught it when Phil Adamson said he found no evidence that Arnold used a cell phone."

"I must be losing my marbles. That should have rung a bell immediately."

As Jill stirred our cappuccino a few minutes later, Jeff called back with the number.

"This should be a big help," I said. "The homicide investigator didn't think Arnold had a cell phone. When we find out who he'd been talking with, maybe it'll give us something to go on."

"Do you have any likely suspects?" Jeff asked.

"Some possibilities, but not one I can pin the tail on. That's what troubles me. I'm pretty sure the murder relates to the case we're working, but there's no clear motive yet."

"Let me know when you find something. Lisle and her sister are getting really uptight over this."

"I'll call you as soon as we find some answers."

I promptly put in a call for Phil, but it went to his voice mail. I left word to get back to me as soon as he could, that it was about Arnold Wechsel's cell phone. I figured that would whet his appetite.

I had better luck finding Buddy Ebsen, the fire investigator, but that was the extent of my luck.

"Did you turn up anything from the wreckage of my Jeep?" I asked.

"Evidence that a blasting cap was used to trigger the bomb. We had figured that anyway. Have you thought of any link to a ham radio operator?"

"Not since I was in Vietnam thirty years ago, and that was just to make a phone call home."

When I told Jill, she gave me a sideways glance. "What did you expect, a miracle?"

"I didn't expect one, but it sure would've been nice to encounter one."

"Why don't we drop by the Jeep dealer's and check out the new Grand Cherokees? I read where this year's model is a complete change from the old one. That'll be your Christmas present."

Sounded good to me. Nothing else was making a lot of sense these days. Of course it created a bit of a dilemma. I still hadn't bought her a present. We had agreed not to buy each other presents, but I figured she'd be disappointed if she didn't get something. We headed off to the nearest Chrysler dealer where, as expected, a glad-handing, eager young salesman accosted us the moment we stepped into the showroom.

"Merry Christmas, folks," he said with a grin as wide as Detroit. "You've come at just the right time for the best deals of the year. What can I show you?"

He was a bit on the hefty side with short brown hair and a predatory look that was like a neon sign shouting "Buyer Beware!"

"Let's see what you have in Grand Cherokees," I said, confident my partner could handle anything he threw at us.

"Come right this way. We have a real beauty in a Limited with a five-point-seven liter Hemi V-8 engine. Got power the old Cherokee could only dream of."

We followed him across the showroom to a shiny red SUV that looked much sharper than my old model.

He launched into his pitch. "Has a new suspension that gives better handling, leans less in corners, and gives a better quality ride. The turning radius is tighter, too. Great in crowded parking lots or driving off-road."

"Does this one have four-wheel drive?" I asked.

"You need four-wheel drive?"

"I do. When you're on surveillance, you need to be able to go anywhere."

His eyes widened. "You follow people? You must be a detective."

"Private investigator."

"Hey, man, that's cool. This one doesn't have four-wheel drive, but we have plenty that do." He moved around to open the hatchback. "Look at all the cargo room. You can put all kinds of surveillance equipment in here. This baby has a lot more room than the old Cherokee. Has power adjustable floor pedals, rain-sensing wipers, adjustable roof rails, eight-way power passenger seat—"

"What about gas mileage?" Jill asked.

"Depends on the engine you choose. Comes in V-Six or V-Eight. The six gets sixteen in the city, twenty-one on the highway. With the eight it's fifteen and twenty."

"Better than I was getting with the old one," I said.

"It comes standard with four-wheel anti-lock disc brakes and a tire pressure monitoring system. You can get it with GPS navigation built into the radio."

I had heard enough. "If you have a Limited in black with all that, I'll take it."

He checked the records and returned with word that they had one ready to go. The price was more than $34,000, but my hard-nosed business manager got a nice chunk knocked off before we signed the deal. When it was all over, we drove back to the office in separate cars. As I was pulling into the shopping center parking area, my cell phone rang.

"I tried your office first," Detective Adamson said. "What's this about a cell phone?"

I steered toward a parking spot beside Jill's car as I told him what Jeff Price had said about the cell phone and what we remembered from the conversation with Arnold's neighbor.

"Damn, Greg. I should have dug a little deeper into that. But there were no financial records—"

"It's pretty safe to say he worked for Nick Zicarelli, probably collected money for him. I'd wager Zicarelli paid him in cash, and Arnold likely paid some of his bills the same way."

"You're sure about old Nick?"

I went over our interrogation, what we'd pried out of him, and Nikki's response.

"I'll get on this cell phone angle and request a log of Wechsel's calls," he said. "I'd have to say Christmas Eve isn't a very good time to accomplish something like this. I have to get a subpoena to start with."

"I understand. We also followed up this morning on the Scotch bottle delivery. It was sent from Nashville by a guy using a fictitious name and address. He used a young man, practically a teenager, to take the package to the delivery outfit. So no description. But he gave a fake address on Sheridan Drive. I've no doubt it was Isabell."

"Probably true, but we need some evidence. I'll check back with the fingerprint techs. They were supposed to send the bottle on to the TBI toxicology lab. I talked to a buddy there who promised to push it, but again, it's Christmas."

The Tennessee Bureau of Investigation crime lab was state of the art. It would be only a matter of time, but time was the problem. Everybody wanted to be off for the holiday.

"Maybe we'll get lucky," I said, not really holding out much hope.

"Thanks for the cell phone tip. Merry Christmas to you and Jill."

I gave him our regards and glanced over at Jill's Camry. I didn't know how she managed to get here before me. I'm usually the fast guy in the family. But seeing her car reminded me of what I needed to do. I detoured by the jewelry store a few doors away and looked for a pin in the shape of a violin sparkling with diamonds. Jill had admired it recently, mainly because of her mother's symphony career, but she thought it way too expensive. I had it gift-wrapped and trudged back through the cold to the office. When I got there, I told Jill that Phil planned to go after the cell phone logs but didn't expect to get any quick results.

"Maybe we should wrap it up here and head for the fireplace, too," she said. "We can put our milk and cookies out for Santa early."

"Hmph," I grunted. "From the looks of his belly, he'd probably rather have beer and pretzels."

"Oh, boy, some nosy elf is sure to pass that on to him."

"Doesn't matter. I've already got my new Grand Cherokee Limited. I'll be warm and comfy while the old guy is freezing his jolly red butt off in a topless sled."

"I think I'll nominate you for the Grinch Award."

When I reached my hand in my inside jacket pocket to see if I'd left the gift receipt there, I felt something else. I pulled out a folded sheet of paper and opened it.

"Dang, I may qualify for that award." I handed her the paper. "Sam gave me this the other night. It's a family the church was contacted about. I said we'd take care of it, but with this case keeping us in a tizzy, I completely forgot."

She read down the list. "Greg, we should've bought this stuff three days ago. There are two kids to buy for, and groceries. The stores close early."

The phone rang. RT Investigations' number showed on the caller ID.

"Getting ready for Santa, Red?" I asked.

"He just came."

"He did?"

"Yeah, in the form of the guy who used to work for Louie Aregis."

"Great. He give you some names of Nashville investors?"

"Five. You want to write them down?"

I grabbed a pen and jotted the names on a pad as he called them out. With number five, I whooped. "Bingo!"

"You know him?" Red asked.

"We just talked to him yesterday. Send me your bill, friend. Our client will happily pay it."

"There's more, but I don't know how you could use it. Remember my FBI friend in New York? He's in Florida now. We were talking yesterday about some money laundering schemes they had run into that involved investment firms.

When I mentioned Aregis's name, he said he couldn't give me any details but Coastal Capital was the target of an investigation."

Jill sat there biting on her lower lip when I put down the phone. "What did he say?"

"Nick Zicarelli is one of Aregis's clients."

She slumped back in her chair. "He's obviously got scads of money, and he's a basketball fanatic. I'll bet he put up the cash for Louie Aregis to buy into the NBA franchise."

"And Arnold found out about it. He got mad when Zicarelli fired him and decided to be a whistleblower."

"If that's true, you know who stood to gain the most by killing Arnold Wechsel," Jill said. She picked up a pencil and twirled it nervously.

The same thought had occurred to me. Nick Zicarelli appeared capable of committing murder, but how would he know Arnold was to meet me at that auto repair shop? The young man was no dummy. I didn't think he would risk leaking his intentions to the guy most likely to take whatever steps necessary to stop him. I had little doubt Arnold planned to tell me that Zicarelli was buying into the NBA franchise by proxy. I suspected the old man had even offered to pay the cost of moving Coastal Capital Ventures to Nashville so he could get in on the deal. Without Arnold to testify, though, we had no proof of anything. As I thought about it, I realized there was another man with just as much to lose if Arnold talked.

"Are you going to call Phil?" Jill asked.

"I would if we had something substantial to give him. Think about it, Jill. Louie Aregis would have as much of a motive to kill Arnold as Zicarelli. And he's short enough to have fired with an upward trajectory like the autopsy showed. By contrast, Zicarelli would appear too tall."

She looked crestfallen. I also reminded her where we stood without Arnold to corroborate.

"At least you should call Terry," she said.

I agreed. After I explained the situation, our client remained silent for a few moments, no doubt mulling over the possibilities.

"I don't handle criminal cases these days," he said, "but I spent a few years in the DA's office after law school. Metro Homicide could pull Zicarelli in, but they wouldn't get far. He's a wily old fox. As soon as they asked more than his name, rank, and serial number, he'd have his lawyer in there. I suspect he doesn't do business over a regular phone, so they'd find nothing going that route."

"And I'm sure he only deals in cash with his gambling patrons."

"True. The money is probably laundered through his real estate activities and then goes into his investment account with Coastal Capital. You'd have to subpoena their records to prove his money was going into the kitty for the basketball project."

"I just learned from a good contact that Coastal Capital is the subject of an FBI money laundering investigation."

"That's good to know," Terry said, "but it probably won't help us. Those investigations can go on for months, even years. We don't have that kind of time."

"What if the newspaper got onto the story, started looking into a Zicarelli-Aregis connection? It might stir up enough questions the NBA commissioner's office would start their own investigation. Maybe decide the possibility of a professional gambler being involved was enough to kill the deal."

"Could you get the newspaper interested?" Terry asked.

"I know a reporter who would probably jump at it."

"Get him jumping."

30

WHEN I TOLD Jill what our client had agreed to, she checked her watch, sighed, and held out the list Sam had given me.

"When are we going to get everything on this list?"

"As soon as we have lunch with our favorite reporter."

I picked up the phone and punched in Wes Knight's number.

"Have you had lunch?" I asked when he came on the line.

"No, I'm taking off early. Slow news day. Nothing much to write about but Christmas stories. All that good news is depressing. The wire services can handle things from here on."

"How would you like a bombshell of a story, my friend?"

"Is this for real or some kind of joke? Seems like I've been dealing with jokers all day."

"How about the possibility of a professional gambler being involved in this NBA franchise deal?"

"Hmm. You asked about Nick Zicarelli the other day. Is he involved?"

"Name somewhere we can buy you a sandwich, and I'll give you the whole story."

"My editor frowns on reporter bribery, but I'll be glad to meet you."

We agreed on an Arby's not far out West End Avenue from the newspaper office. I turned to Jill. "As soon as we finish with Wes, we'll go on a shopping spree."

When we got to the restaurant, Jill suggested splitting a

turkey and Swiss sandwich. A half was a decent size, though I would have preferred to tackle the whole thing by myself. I placed the order and we took our coffee to a booth by the window. I saw Wes and waved as he headed for the entrance. When he joined us with a milk shake and a sandwich piled high with roast beef, I decided I hated Wes Knight. I had to admit, though, that thanks to Jill's efforts, he made me look almost slim. He was a big man with a full face and a small beard that reminded me of Burl Ives.

"How'd you get your order so quickly and we have to wait?" I asked.

"Privilege of the press," he said. "Plus I'm a regular here, and I know what to ask for that they keep ready."

"I'll have to remember that," I said.

He siphoned the foam off his shake. "Okay, give me the lowdown on this deal."

"First, you have to agree to leave us out of it," I said. "I'll give you some sources, but we don't want to be connected with the story. Agreed?"

He put his elbows on the table and tapped his fingertips. "Why don't you want any credit?"

"It's a confidentiality thing."

"How so?"

"We're working a case where the client requires that he remain anonymous. If you used our name, it would put us in the spotlight and might compromise him."

"Now you're sounding like James Bond."

Sometimes you have to humor people. "Matter of fact, Jill had to go undercover last night."

He looked at Jill and grinned. "The lady's got talent. Okay, if I can nail things down without dragging you in, it's a deal."

"You can. Here's the story in capsule. Nick Zicarelli is an investor with Louie Aregis's Coastal Capital Ventures. One of his former employees in Florida says Aregis moved his business to Nashville because of the NBA deal. We think Zicarelli brought him here. Knowing Nick's passion for NBA basketball, we believe he's financing Coastal Capital's involvement."

"Who's going to confirm all this?"

"I'll put you in touch with a private investigator in Pensacola, where Aregis came from. He's been in contact with the former employee."

"You say you believe Zicarelli is financing the deal. Anyway to know for sure?"

I grinned. "With your bird-dogging reputation, I figure you can sniff that out from Aregis or Zicarelli or some other contact. We know Aregis has lied about the way he got into the deal. He claimed the local guys approached him about getting involved, that he moved to Nashville because he had good clients here and it was a growing city with lots of wealth."

"Don't forget his wife," Jill said.

"Oh, yeah. Reason number three was that she's a big country music fan."

"Yee, haw," Wes said as the loud speaker called out the number for our order.

When I brought our food back to the booth, Jill looked up at me. "Wes wants to know why Zicarelli should be financing the NBA team instead of Aregis himself?"

I turned the tray so Jill could get her half of the sandwich. "The ex-employee down in Florida says Coastal Capital Ventures has lost some important clients lately and hasn't been doing too well. He doesn't think Aregis has the personal funds to shell out a lot of money, and a major sports franchise isn't the type of cash cow investors in a venture capital firm would appreciate."

"Makes sense," Wes said, and took a big bite of roast beef.

"Also, a man connected to one of the other local partners

told a friend of mine that Aegis heard about the deal somehow and contacted them about getting involved. I suspect he heard about it from Zicarelli."

"I'll see if I can confirm that," Wes said. He chewed a moment, then looked across at me with a raised eyebrow. "What's the scoop on your car bomb episode?"

It wasn't a question I'd expected, but I fielded it with aplomb. "The fire investigator hasn't found anything that points toward who's responsible. I got a new Jeep Grand Cherokee out of it, though. The black one over there." I pointed out the window.

"Looks nice," he said. "Any new developments on that murder case where you found the victim?"

I should have known I'd get the third degree on the whole litany of matters I was involved in. That was the risk you took when dealing with reporters. I thought about telling him our belief that Arnold had worked for Zicarelli but decided I'd best leave that one alone.

"You'll need to talk to Detective Adamson about that," I said. "He doesn't confide in me all that often."

"That so? After that assassination case a few months back, I thought the three of you were thick as thieves, as my sainted mother would put it."

"I doubt that Phil Adamson would use that simile," Jill said with a broad smile.

"Okay. Thanks for the tip about Zicarelli," Wes said. "I'll get right on it. Probably won't make my wife too happy, Christmas being tomorrow. I'm scheduled to work a few hours on the holiday anyway, though we got most of the Sunday paper done today."

We swapped Christmas wishes shortly afterward. Wes headed back to the office and we started the drive to Hermitage. On the way we stopped first at a clothing store for white boots, a scarf, and a wool cap for a ten-year-old girl named Brenda. In the boys' section, we chose blue jeans and a red shirt for Larry, a boy of eight. It wasn't on the list, but Jill picked out a handbag for June, the mother.

At a toy store, we found the requested games, a remote-controlled car, and a doll-size version of a tea set. We tossed in a couple of books for good measure. Then it was off to the grocery for a turkey breast, a sliced ham, and a variety of vegetables and fruits.

"I wish I'd known earlier," Jill said. "I'd have cooked up a nice dessert for them."

Instead, we chose a cake and cookies and added in packets of hot chocolate and apple cider. We stopped by the office to pick up Jill's car and headed home, where she quickly wrapped the gifts.

WITH WINTER IN its infancy, daylight disappeared early. The outside floodlights substituted for the missing sun, however, as I moved the Jeep near the front porch and carried everything out to stow it in the cargo area. I checked around the lawn and driveway. Everything looked normal. I put the address in my new GPS, feeling like Santa in his sleigh, and off we went in search of the young mother's house. Following the satellite-directed turns, we found it in a less plush section of Hermitage, on a street filled with duplexes, some bearing For Rent signs, one with the last tenant's battered sofa and assorted belongings dumped at the front of the lot. It was a tough time for an eviction.

Jill glanced at the note with all the info. "Her name's June Everly. I can't imagine what it would be like having to face Christmas with so little for the kids, depending on the goodness of strangers."

The Everly's side of the duplex looked neat, with no papers or trash scattered about the lawn. A vintage blue Ford with a weather-mottled paint job sat in the driveway. A simple green wreath with a red bow hung on the door. It appeared to be one of the better-kept examples of low-rent America. I parked behind the Ford, and we gathered up the bags and carried them to the house.

A woman of around thirty, sandy hair pulled back and tied with a scrunchie, opened the door. She wore jeans and a brown sweater, flip-flops on her feet. A friendly smile brightened her round face. In an earlier era, she would have made a great model for a Norman Rockwell cover.

"We're Greg and Jill McKenzie from Gethsemane United Methodist Church," I said. "We have a few things for you."

"Oh, my goodness." She stared in awe. "Please come in."

As we walked into the small living room, I saw a short but gaily-decorated Christmas tree. There was also a floor lamp, a sofa and chair, a nineteen-inch TV, and a few toys scattered about. Jill set the shopping bag filled with gifts by the sofa as a wide-eyed boy and girl stuck their heads out of the kitchen.

"You must be Brenda and Larry," Jill said. "Merry Christmas."

"These are the McKenzies, kids," June Everly said. "They brought us lots of nice things."

They both waved and I turned to Mrs. Everly. "These are groceries. Should I put them in the kitchen."

"Forgive my manners," she said, a bit flustered. "Let me help you."

She took the smaller bag and led me into the kitchen, which appeared adequate though only a fraction of the size of Jill's.

"You can leave the turkey out for awhile," Jill said, "then put it in the refrigerator. It should thaw enough to cook tomorrow."

"I'm overwhelmed," the young mother said, shaking her head.

I looked around at the kids, who were watching every move. "Do you want to save the presents until in the morning, or open them now?"

They glanced at each other and said "Now" in unison.

We sat on the sofa while they pulled out packages and ripped off the wrapping.

"I hate to tear up such pretty paper," Mrs. Everly said as she gently slit open her box. "Oh, what a pretty bag. I needed a new one. This is just perfect."

The kids squealed in excitement as they pulled out their toys and new clothes. "Thank you, thank you," little Brenda said repeatedly.

"Can I get you something to drink?" Mrs. Everly asked. "We have tea and Coke."

"We appreciate the offer, but no thanks," Jill said. "We'll be eating supper when we get home."

The young mother followed us to the door as we left, thanking us profusely. "You've made this a wonderful Christmas for us," she said. "I feel like you were sent by God."

I felt humbled and ashamed for having almost forgotten.

"Seeing the joy in these youngsters' eyes makes it all worthwhile," Jill said. "You and Brenda and Larry have a great Christmas and a wonderful New Year."

In the car, Jill leaned over and kissed me on the cheek. I pulled her closer and made it a real smooch.

"I feel like we've had our Christmas," she said. "Anything that happens tomorrow will seem anticlimactic."

I knew what she meant, but I also knew that predictions about the future were fraught with the potential for miscalculation.

● 31

WE SAT AT THE kitchen table feeling pleasantly stuffed when Phil called.

"There were no prints on the bottle except yours," he said. "He evidently wore gloves, which was a wise move if he was dealing with cyanide. However, he wasn't so smart with the package. Evidently he didn't know we could lift prints from paper. There were several prints, with you and the delivery people handling it, but they found enough to make a positive ID through AFIS of former federal prison inmate Izzy Isabell."

The FBI's Automated Fingerprint Identification System was a priceless asset.

"Now all we need is confirmation on the Scotch," I said.

"I'll contact my buddy again and see where that stands. I considered hauling Isabell in on some minor charge so we could keep him on ice until the tox results are in, but the DA wouldn't buy it. East Precinct reported the blue pickup is still parked in the driveway on Sheridan Drive. We may have to put a tail on him to be sure he doesn't run."

When I gave Jill the news, she proceeded to put it all in perspective.

"That means we don't have to worry about the lieutenant for the time being," she said. "Now if we could just figure out who the bomber was..."

She let it slide, but she'd said enough.

A short time later, the outside floodlight warning sounded.

When I looked out this time, I saw what appeared to be a GMC Yukon SUV pulling up to the house. A large man wearing a black leather jacket and a leather cap climbed out, reached across the seat for a package, and walked toward the house. Having learned to be overly cautious, I turned to Jill, who had followed me to the living room.

"Grab your pistol and keep it handy, just in case."

She hurried back to the office where she had left her purse.

I waited for the doorbell, then opened the door. The man stood around six-two, well over 200 pounds. He smiled and tipped his cap back. I saw the package was gift wrapped with bright Christmas paper. The security door remained closed, though the upper window pane was open.

"Mr. McKenzie?" he asked in a deep voice.

I nodded. "What can I do for you?"

"I'm Barley," he said. "Mr. Nick Zicarelli asked me to bring you this little package, sort of a token of his respect."

I frowned. "What's the occasion?"

"He said he wants you to know there's no hard feelings. There may have been some misunderstandings. Mr. Nick is a really compassionate man, but sometimes, when he gets upset, he says things that may not sound quite like what he meant."

I had no doubt about what he meant when he shouted "Hell, no!" at me. Apparently Nikki was convinced of the way he sounded when he called her. This was an interesting exercise, but I wasn't quite ready to take it at face value.

"Is this his way of apologizing?" I asked.

Barley gave a little twist to his head that seemed to indicate uncertainty. "He just wants to leave things in a more friendly manner. Keep it amiable, you know."

"I have no problem with that." I turned the dead bolt and pushed the security door open. "Come on in and open it for me," I said.

His dark eyes flashed as if he'd been hit by an electric current. Then his face relaxed into the beginnings of a smile. "Oh, I get it. You think...that's funny. Mr. Nick will get a big laugh out of that."

"If you'd just had your car blown up with you inside, it wouldn't sound so funny," I said.

"I guess not." He nodded. "Mr. Nick told me about that."

So Mr. Nick was well aware of who I was and what I had been doing.

Barley came in and I pointed toward the table beside the sofa. "You can open it there."

He shrugged, tore off the Christmas wrap, and removed the lid from a large box. It was filled with Ghiardelli chocolates.

Jill walked over and stared at it. "That's enough to last us for a year."

Barley grinned. "Well, enjoy it, folks. I need to be on my way."

When he left, I picked up a chocolate and sniffed at it. "Don't detect any bitter almonds, so I don't guess it's laced with cyanide."

"You don't really think he would send us tainted chocolates, do you?" Jill asked.

"No, but I'm not sure just what he's up to. Maybe he's trying to open the door to the possibility of manipulating our investigation. Like Terry said earlier, he's a wily old fox."

SINCE MOVING TO Hermitage, we had made a tradition of attending the midnight Christmas Eve service at Gethsemane United Methodist Church. Actually, it started at eleven and wound up around midnight. We always sat with Sam and Wilma Gannon and several other members of the Sunday School class. The service by candlelight lent a feeling of lapsing back 2000 years to the biblical origin of the celebration.

Some of our classmates had already taken their seats by the time we arrived shortly before eleven. I sat beside John Jernigan, an accountant who had retired from what was now known as U.S. Smokeless Tobacco. It was the maker of the famous Bruton's Snuff, and John had been stuck with the nickname "Snuffy" in earlier times. We honored his desire to be known by his given name. He was a confirmed smoker and his tobacco expertise had helped us out with the Marathon Motor Works case a few months ago.

"What have you been up to, Greg?" he asked.

"Trying to make a buck the usual way."

"I read about you finding that young fellow who'd been shot over in Northeast Nashville last week."

"That was a real shocker. I guess you also heard about my Jeep getting barbequed."

"Sam told me. Any idea who did it?"

"No, the investigators are still working on it. How about you? How's your holiday season going?"

"Ha. You know us retired guys don't get holidays. I've been spending a lot of time on my ham radio rig, trying to see how many countries I can reach. Gotten a pretty good list so far."

"I didn't know you were a ham, John." I gave him a curious look. "You never mentioned it."

"I sort of got away from it for several years. Recently I decided to update my equipment and give it another try. Keeps me out of pool rooms."

I laughed and was about to ask him the question that had been bugging me lately, but the service started before I could get to it. We sang all the familiar Christmas hymns, the choir performed a beautiful anthem, and one of the members with a great voice read the scriptural account of Christ's birth. Dr. Peter Trent, our pastor, told the story of Henry Wadsworth Longfellow's troubled life that led to his writing the poem that became the Christmas carol "I Heard the Bells on Christmas Day." The carol typified the spirit of the season with its message of peace on earth, good will to men. Thinking about Arnold's murder, I knew somebody out there had missed the message. I was even more determined to track him down and bring him to account.

When the lights came on in the sanctuary, everybody began to bundle up for the trek out into the frigid night. I finally had the chance to put my question to John Jernigan.

"You must know a lot of local hams," I said. "Do you by chance know one who drives a Cadillac Escalade?"

He cocked his head as he pulled on a heavy jacket. "No, can't say that I do. Of course, I haven't been back into it for all that long. Who're you looking for?"

I chuckled. "I'm not sure. Just taking a shot in hopes of hitting something. The investigators found evidence that a handheld transceiver like the ones used by ham operators was used to trigger the bomb that did in my Jeep. They wanted to know if I knew any hams. I told them I hadn't run into one since I made a phone call home from Vietnam."

"Then you used somebody with the Military Amateur Radio Service. Some of those GI's did miraculous things setting up stations in combat zones. They cannibalized stuff to put it all together so people could make calls to their kinfolks back home."

"Yeah. That was back in the days when making an overseas call was a big deal. Were you involved in the Amateur Radio Service?"

"Sure was. Got a cigarette lighter to prove it."

He pulled a Zippo lighter from his pocket and showed it to me. I saw a round symbol with a globe and the letters "MARS." Printed in a circle around the globe was "Military Amateur Radio Service."

My breathing quickened as it hit me. "Do you know a CPA named Gordon Franklin?"

"Sure." He grinned. "He was a MARS operator in Vietnam. Did you run into him over there?"

Before I could answer, Jill tugged at my sleeve. "Let's go, Greg, so they can lock up the church."

I turned to Jernigan. "Thanks, John. See you Sunday."

When we got outside, Jill asked, "What were you and John palavering about?"

"Remember the paperweight on Gordon Franklin's desk that had M-A-R-S on it? It stands for Military Amateur Radio Service. One of the Protect Our Preds is a ham radio operator. You know what Buddy Ebsen said about the bomb maker. Franklin's a short guy. It could have been Franklin instead of Frank that Arnold Wechsel's neighbor heard him saying in an angry voice on his cell phone."

"Why in the world would Gordon Franklin want us out of the way, not to mention Arnold?"

"That's what we need to find out."

"Aren't you sort of jumping to conclusions?"

"I'll have to admit it's a long shot, nothing more than a hunch at this stage. But put all of it together and who knows? Sometimes hunches pay off."

"Okay. Then I suppose you want to find what kind of car Franklin drives?"

"Exactly."

I pulled out my cell phone and punched in Phil Adamson's number. I got a drowsy sounding "Hello."

"Phil, it's Greg McKenzie."

"Damn." After a pause, he said, "Do you know what time it is? Who's dead now?"

I glanced at my watch. "It's Christmas morning, Phil. Merry Christmas. I need a favor."

"Christ a'mighty, Greg. Can't it wait till daylight?"

"We may have found the car bomber, and he could be the man we're looking for."

"Slow down. Do you have any evidence, or is this more speculation?"

"You're always getting technical."

"I have laws to follow."

"Consider this one the law of preservation."

"What's happened?"

"We don't have a case ready for the grand jury, but we have enough to warrant some serious probing."

I told him briefly the reasons behind my suspicions, then asked if he could find out what kind of car Franklin drove. "If he has a Cadillac Escalade, I need to have a talk with that gentleman."

"Go to bed, Greg. I'll check it out in the morning."

●⌐ **32**

WE SLEPT LATE on Christmas morning. Both of our parents had died years ago, and neither of us had siblings or aunts and uncles to visit. Jill had discovered a couple of younger generation cousins as the result of an investigation we had worked back in the spring. She kept in touch with Molly Harrison, who had taken back her maiden name after the tragic end of the case. Interested in maintaining family ties, Jill invited her over for Christmas dinner, but she had already made other plans.

When we rolled out of bed, I suggested we check under the Christmas tree and see what Santa had brought.

She gave me a knowing grin. "What have you done, Greg? I thought we made a pact not to buy each other gifts."

"I got a new Grand Cherokee."

"All right. Let's check it out."

We went downstairs in our PJ's. With the drapes closed and a thick overcast outside, the living room resembled nighttime. I switched on the tree lights and lit the logs in the fireplace. When I turned around, Jill sat on the floor in front of the tree, holding the small package.

I grinned. "Open it."

She peeled off the wrapping and lifted the lid off the box. She caught her breath. "Greg, you shouldn't have."

"You don't like it?"

"I love it, but it was so—"

"So what? It'll look great on you. That's all that counts."

I sat beside her and she reached around, pulled me toward her, gave me a monstrous kiss. "I love you," she said.

"And I love you, babe."

With a gentle movement, I laid her back on the carpet. I felt the warmth from the fire on my back and saw the reflection of the flames dancing in her eyes.

"When was the last time you made love in front of a Christmas tree?" I asked.

"I don't think we ever did that." She grinned. "But there's no time like the present."

It was after ten o'clock when we sat at the kitchen table with cups of cappuccino and strawberry muffins.

"I wish Phil would call," I said, checking my watch.

"Give him a break. He's probably got family over to open presents."

"This is no time to be monkeying around with toys."

She munched on a muffin, then said, "Have you come up with any reason Gordon Franklin would want to kill Arnold? The young man was apparently intent on exposing something that would thwart the NBA plans. That's exactly what the Protect Our Preds people want."

"I know. And I haven't figured it out. It doesn't make much sense, does it?"

"I can't really see Nick Zicarelli murdering Arnold, either. He could have hired someone to do it, though."

"It might make more sense for Louie Aregis to have done it," I said. "But how would he know what Arnold planned to do, or where and when he would meet me?"

"I think we may have to sit down with Phil and lay out everything we know. He has the resources to look into all these questions."

I hated to admit she was right, but it didn't appear that we had the clout to go after these people.

When the phone finally rang, I hesitated. Jill got up and answered it. "He's right here, Phil."

I took the phone. "What did you find?"

"Sorry, pal, but there's no Cadillac Escalade registered to Gordon Franklin."

"Bummer," I said.

"As a matter of fact, there are no vehicles at all registered in Franklin's name."

"But he's bound to drive something."

"I checked Franklin, Gretchen and Silverman. It's not theirs. Of course, he could drive a leased car and that wouldn't show."

I felt a bit deflated, and I guess my voice showed it. "Thanks, Phil. I apologize for waking you up last night."

"Don't feel too bad. I've followed more than my share of false leads. Anyway, I saved the best for last."

"You saved what?"

"My TBI crime lab buddy just called. He's a real conscientious guy. After I told him last night about finding Isabell's fingerprints on the package, he went in this morning and ran the test. That bottle of Scotch contained enough potassium cyanide that you'd be a Christmas cadaver if you'd celebrated with it."

"Damn, Phil." This was one Christmas I wouldn't likely forget.

Looking across at my expression, Jill had no response to my expletive.

"I'm getting ready to go out and pick him up," Phil said. "We haven't been watching him, but who runs on Christmas Eve, especially since he thinks he's safe?"

"Give him my regards," I said.

Jill looked across at me as I switched off the phone. "What happened?"

"The Scotch tested positive for cyanide. If I hadn't been curious about that tax stamp, we'd be the late McKenzies."

She opened her mouth as if to say something, then closed it, shaking her head. "Thank God for curiosity," she murmured.

"Phil has gone after Izzy."

"What did he say about the Cadillac Escalade?"

"He didn't find anything," I said. "Franklin doesn't have any kind of car registered in his name, but it could be a lease."

She thought about that for a moment. "You've been wanting to show me how to do a stakeout in a situation like this. Here's your chance."

"Y'know, you're a doll," I said with a smile and blew her a kiss. "We can park on the street and look like Aunt Susie and Uncle Nabob visiting for Christmas. Perfect setup."

WE TOOK JILL'S Camry, figuring it would be less obvious. Franklin's house sat on a tree-lined street not far off Hillsboro Road. A two-story brick, it didn't appear all that ostentatious. I suspected it was his old family home. It had a large lawn and a paved driveway that led back to a free-standing white wooden garage. I parked on the opposite side of the street, a couple of houses down, with a clear view of the garage.

Jill had packed bottles of water and snacks. We settled in around eleven-thirty, taking turns at keeping an eye on the Franklin house. The one not "on duty" passed the time by reading a mystery novel selected from our formidable to-be-read book pile. After a while, the windows began to fog like a night at the seashore.

Working lookout at the time, I turned to Jill. "Could you go a little easier on the breathing? I'm having difficulty seeing the driveway."

She gave me the evil eye, took out a tissue, and wiped the inside of the windshield.

"Thanks," I said as she returned to her reading.

With everybody but us enjoying their Christmas dinner, the street looked about as lively as the home stretch at a turtle race. I counted one car going in each direction during my hour of gazing. I was about to prompt Jill to put down her book when she looked around.

"I think you'd better run the engine a bit and warm us up," she said. "My nose is starting to look like Rudolph's."

A little sunshine would have been helpful, but the sky remained as gray as grandma's shawl. I turned the switch and cranked the starter. "Okay," I said, "it's your turn to be watchman."

I adjusted the heater to its highest level and she dropped her book on the console.

"How long do we need to keep this up?" she asked.

"Until we get some results. Either he goes out or he comes in, and we get a look at what he's driving. He may have gone to spend the day with his brother in Murfreesboro. I warned you this was the most monotonous part of an investigator's life."

She pulled out her goodie bag. "I made some small sandwiches. You have your choice of chicken salad or pimiento cheese."

I chose to eat more chicken. After a couple of hours, I spotted a Metro patrol car approaching us slowly from the rear. "Here comes trouble," I said. "That's one of the hazards of surveillance in an upscale neighborhood."

The car pulled in behind us. The officer got out and walked toward us. I lowered my window and held out my PI card.

"We're on a surveillance job," I said. I added a smile to keep it light. "Your presence isn't helping our cause."

"A neighbor behind you called about a suspicious car parked on the street with two people in it," he said.

"Tell them our car broke down and the tow truck is coming from California."

"Brilliant." He shook his head. He looked fairly young, not too jaded yet, his thick mop of brown hair picked at by the chilling breeze. "Who's the subject?"

"Guy who lives over there." I pointed toward Franklin's house. "He hasn't poked his head out so far. Maybe he thinks he's a groundhog and it isn't February yet."

"As cold as it is, he'll stay inside if he's smart. I'll tell the people who called that you're okay. If we get any more complaints, though, you'll have to move along."

The Camry's heater kept the chill at bay, though we used a lot of gas to keep it fired up. No more cops snooped around. A little after four, as colors began to fade with the gathering darkness, I looked in the rearview mirror and saw the headlights of a car coming up from behind. It slowed just past us and turned into Franklin's driveway.

"It's a dark blue Lincoln Navigator," Jill said, almost a whisper.

We had been wrong about the make and model of the vehicle, or about the role of Gordon Franklin. I wasn't sure which.

I cranked the starter and drove off.

33

"I KNOW THAT look," Jill said as I turned toward Hillsboro Road. "You wanted to go after him, didn't you?"

"Yes, but it looks like we need to re-evaluate."

"We know for certain that Fred Ricketts drives a Cadillac Escalade."

"Yes," I said, "but I'm not so sure what we saw originally was an Escalade. It could easily have been a Navigator."

"What do you suggest we do now?"

"If we were on a football field, we'd punt and hope the other team would fumble or make some equally stupid mistake."

"And since we aren't?"

"We go home and try to come up with a better idea."

Neither of us spoke much on the way. I ran over all the possibilities in my mind, and I suspect Jill did the same. I was no closer to an answer when we arrived home.

Jill suggested we eat supper and follow it with a brainstorming session. Since my brain appeared to have taken a holiday, I had nothing better to propose. We weren't in the mood for turkey and dressing and all the usual Yuletide trappings. She baked chicken breasts in a mixture of wine and spices and served it with peas, carrots, and a green salad. It was simple fare but delicious. I volunteered to clean off the table and waited while she loaded the dishwasher.

"How about a little cappuccino to get our gray matter stirring?" Jill asked.

"My old brain needs something to get it working," I said.

Jill got a ruled pad and brought our travel cups filled with the steaming French Vanilla-flavored brew. "Where do we start?"

"Turn your pad sideways and write five names across the top: Arnold Wechsel, Gordon Franklin, Louie Aregis, Fred Ricketts, and Nick Zicarelli. Then we'll list what we know that might tie them together."

While we were in the midst of that exercise, the phone rang. I strode to the counter and answered it.

"This is Gordon Franklin, Mr. McKenzie," he said in his usual unexpressive voice.

Startled, I looked across at Jill, frowning. "Well, hello, Mr. Franklin. How are you?"

"Fine, thanks. I've come across something you need to know about. Could you meet me at my office in half an hour?"

"Certainly." Recalling the problem I'd had with a similar request from Arnold Wechsel, I added, "What does it concern."

"It's sort of complicated," he said. "I really need to explain it in person."

I didn't like being left in the dark, and I had serious reservations about how far to trust the man. There was no way to find out except to go along with him.

"We'll be there," I said.

"Good. I'll leave the front door unlocked. Just come on in to my office."

"Be where?" Jill asked when I put the phone down.

I repeated what Franklin had said.

"What do you suppose he has?" she asked.

"I can't imagine. I'm not sure what to make of it."

She picked up our cups and carried them to the sink. She turned, a wary look on her face. "Do you think there's still a chance he's the one who tried to blow us up?"

"It's a definite possibility. I don't want to put you in any jeopardy. Why don't you stay here?"

"Forget it, Greg. If you're going, I'm going."

I knew there was no use arguing. "We need to be prepared for anything," I said. "Be sure your .38 is loaded. I'll carry my Sig and put the micro voice recorder in my pocket."

We bundled up against the cold and headed out. It had been cloudy all day, and the night was moonless. Virtually deserted, the streets looked dark and ominous. The possibilities of what we might find made a jumble of my thoughts as I drove. It took barely twenty minutes to reach the offices of Franklin, Gretchen and Silverman. I parked beside the Navigator. In the dark, I decided it could easily have been the vehicle we saw Sunday night. As we entered the building, I switched on the recorder.

Franklin met us when we walked into the office suite. His subtle smile seemed about as natural as a platinum blonde.

"You can put your jackets here," he said, indicating a coat rack in the reception area.

"Thanks," I said. "We're okay." I didn't want to show my holster.

He shrugged. "As you wish."

He led us back to his office, where two chairs sat in front of the desk. He moved around to his leather chair and we took our seats.

"You have us quite intrigued, Mr. Franklin," I said. "What have you found?"

He sat back in the chair, elbows on the arms, and steepled his fingers. Although his body was on the stocky side, his fingers looked more like those of a pianist. He wore an open-collar white dress shirt and a yellow cardigan, giving him something of a professorial air. An expensive gold pen lay on the desk in front of him.

"This young fellow whose body you found last week," he said, his eyes fixed on me, "I think I encountered him recently."

"Arnold Wechsel?"

"Yes." He picked up the pen and began twisting it slowly between his fingers. "I was looking for something in a stack of newspapers and came across a picture of him. I recognized it as the man who came by here recently."

"Wechsel was here?"

"Our building is owned by Zicarelli Properties. He came by to pick up the rent. They must have been having problems with the mail."

I glanced at Jill, whose puzzled look was no different than my own. "Did you talk to him?"

"No. I just happened to be out in the reception area when he came in."

"I'm a little curious as to why you thought we would be interested in knowing this?"

He leaned forward, opened the desk drawer and dropped the pen inside. That disinterested look he had displayed at our first interview was replaced by the expression of a man on a mission. "You had asked if I knew the man. I wanted to set the record straight. Brad Smotherman told me you thought Wechsel might be collecting gambling debts for Mr. Zicarelli. I thought you'd like to know it was rent he collected."

"Uh, Greg," Jill said, "we didn't tell Brad Smotherman we suspected Arnold was collecting gambling debts."

I met Franklin's gaze. His eyes had turned as cold as the night outside. "She's right, Mr. Franklin. The only person who had any inkling that we suspected Arnold Wechsel of collecting gambling money was Nick Zicarelli. What we told Brad about was our suspicions regarding Zicarelli's funding Louie Aregis's part of the NBA franchise deal."

The pieces all suddenly fell together. Arnold had collected

bets from Franklin. Somehow Arnold found out about our investigation from the CPA, and Franklin learned the young man planned to meet me Saturday night at Pete Lara's repair shop.

"I think you're mistaken," Franklin said.

His right hand rested on the open drawer. I suspected the worst as he started to lift it. I pushed my jacket aside and reached for my Sig. Before I could get it out, he had a 9mm Glock pointed at my head.

"Hold it right there," he said in as menacing a voice as I'd heard lately.

I should have been ready for this. I sat there as angry at myself as at him.

"You talked to Arnold and found out he planned to meet me," I said. "You got there before I did and killed him. Why?"

Franklin's expression never changed. "He intended to tell you that Nick provided the money for Aregis to buy into the basketball franchise. If they'd have dug into Nick's gambling operation, they'd no doubt have turned up all the bets I've placed with him. That would've ruined my business. I couldn't take a chance on that."

I recalled Smotherman's comment that it would kill Franklin if anything happened to his accounting practice.

"Zicarelli had fired Arnold," I said. "How did you happen to tell him about me?"

"Nick is super-cautious. He doesn't depend on the mail or telephones. He uses people like Wechsel to take bets and handle payoffs. When I called the young man to meet me for a large bet I wanted to place, he told me he'd been fired. He was mad as hell and wanted to get even. He'd overheard Nick talking about funding Coastal Capital's efforts toward an NBA team. I told him a private investigator was looking for ways to botch the deal. I suggested he set up a meeting with you at seven-thirty, when Pete Lara's place would be dark and deserted. That's where we always met."

"You took his cell phone, didn't you?"

He nodded with a look of satisfaction. "I was afraid my phone number would be on his call list."

"And you hoped I would be accused of the murder, didn't you?"

"That was the idea, but you're apparently too clever for that. My little IED didn't work either. I don't know how you escaped the doctored Scotch, but I got my share of Charlies with an M-16 in Nam, and this Glock is capable of doing just as good a job in the U.S. of A."

A shot suddenly rang out beside me. A bullet tore through the front of Franklin's desk, missing him. A quick glance told me Jill had shoved her hand inside her purse and fired her small revolver. Realizing what had happened, a startled look on his face, Franklin turned the semiautomatic toward her.

34

MY LAW ENFORCEMENT training kicked in and I reacted. The moment Franklin shifted his attention to Jill, I pulled my Sig. I swung it up in one swift motion and clamped my left hand against it as I squeezed off two rounds. He pulled the trigger on the Glock as the first bullet hit him. His shot went wild, striking the wall behind us. Two holes appeared in his sweater.

The look of surprise he had showed moments ago seemed frozen in place. He dropped the gun and slumped onto the desk

I leaped up and swept the weapon out of his reach, just in case.

Jill moved in behind me. "Is he...?"

I felt for a pulse. It was weak. "He's alive for now."

I took out my cell phone, punched in 911, and reported a man shot at Franklin, Gretchen, and Silverman. Then I called Phil Adamson.

"You'd better get over to Gordon Franklin's office," I said, breathing hard, the adrenaline still surging.

"What for?"

"I just shot him."

"You what?"

"He's our man. I have him on tape admitting to Arnold Wechsel's murder. He threatened us and pointed a Glock at Jill."

"Is he dead?"

"Not yet. I called for the medics."

"Sit tight. I'm on the way."

The ambulance arrived shortly, as did a couple of cops. Franklin was in shock and bleeding internally. The paramedics rushed him off to the hospital.

"Who shot him?" asked a burly cop with short brown hair and alert blue eyes.

"I did," I said. "He threatened to kill us and fired that Glock on the desk at my wife. We're private investigators."

He looked around at Jill, who had returned to her chair. "You his wife?"

"Yes, sir," she said. "Greg has it all on his digital recorder."

He turned back to me. "Where's your weapon?"

I pulled my jacked aside to show the Sig in its holster. "I planned to give it to Homicide Detective Phil Adamson. He's on the way."

The big cop grinned. "Just for my comfort, how about laying it on the desk there?"

I lifted my gun gingerly from the holster and placed it beside Franklin's Glock.

The other cop, a shorter man with a boyish face that made him look like a new recruit, had been examining the front of the desk. "What happened here?" he asked, pointing to the splintered hole.

"That was my attempt to distract him so Greg could get to his gun," Jill said. She took out the snub-nosed .38 and showed the hole in the end of her bag. "He was concentrating so closely on Greg that he didn't notice when I stuck my hand in here."

I was proud of her. She displayed the coolness of a veteran cop. Before I could say anything else, my cell phone rang.

"You got company?" Phil asked.

"Two officers," I said. "The ambulance took Franklin to the hospital. Vanderbilt, I think."

"Let me talk to one of the officers."

I handed the phone to the big cop. "Detective Adamson wants to talk to you."

He listened a minute, then handed the phone back. "Get back to the entrance," he told the younger officer. "Don't let anybody in till Adamson gets here."

It was another ten minutes before Phil arrived. He was talking on his cell phone when he walked in. Jill and I and the big cop, who we now knew as Officer Bruce Vogel, sat chatting about a similar case he had been involved in. Phil snapped the phone shut and gave me a look I took as a precursor to bad news.

"It's definitely my case now. Franklin didn't make it. Bled out from internal hemorrhage."

I shook my head. Better him than Jill, but it wasn't what I had hoped for. "There's my Sig on the desk. Two shots fired."

"And you got him on tape?"

"Digital," I said.

I took out the mini-recorder and pressed the play button. Since the recorder was voice-activated, there were no sound gaps. It quickly reached the point where Franklin claimed we had told Brad Smotherman we suspected Nick Zicarelli was using Arnold Wechsel to collect gambling debts.

"Who is Brad Smotherman?"

The sharp tone in Phil's voice prompted me to press the STOP button. "He runs Hatrick Brake Company," I said. "Terry Tremont hired us to look into this NBA deal on behalf of an organization bankrolled by Smotherman, Gordon Franklin, and Mack Nelson, the country music star. They're super-fans of the Predators."

"How come you didn't tell me you suspected Wechsel was collecting gambling debts for Nick?"

"We didn't tell that to anybody," I said. "Listen to the recording."

When it ended with the sound of guns firing, Phil looked across at me. "I counted four shots."

"Jill fired first," I said, pointing to the hole in the desk. "I fired twice, and Franklin's shot hit the wall over there."

He looked around, then leaned against the desk. "You were determined it was Franklin, weren't you?"

"Yeah, in the end I guess I was. Zicarelli and Aregis had good reasons to be the killer, but they had no way of knowing I was on the case."

We were interrupted by the arrival of the crime scene crew. Phil briefed them on the situation, then moved aside as they began shooting pictures and gathering evidence, including the bullet lodged in the wall.

Phil turned back to me. ""Franklin apparently put your boy Izzy up to sending the bottle of Scotch. How do you suppose he knew about Isabell?"

I'd wondered about that, too. "My guess is he got the details from Terry Tremont. I told Terry about Isabell because he was complicating my efforts."

"You must have given plenty of detail for him to be able to locate the guy."

"I'm sure I mentioned Nat Edge on Sheridan Road. I guess Franklin could've gotten a phone number out of the book."

"Isabell denied everything when we picked him up. I suspect he'll change his tune now." Phil suddenly grinned like he'd had a wicked vision. "I was ready to send for the shrinks when you called early this morning about that Cadillac."

"Turned out we were wrong," I said. "He drives a Lincoln Navigator."

The grin faded. "Not any more, he doesn't. I'm sure Wechsel's mother will think he got what he deserved."

I was of the same mind. "I promised to let Jeff Price know what happened so he can tell her. She's his sister-in-law."

Phil looked around at Officer Vogel. "That about does it for here, Bruce. Don't know about you, but I'd like to go home and play with the toys Santa brought me."

"I guess you want my toys," I said, holding out the recorder.

Phil dropped it in an evidence bag and placed my Sig and Franklin's Glock in two others. "I'll get yours back to you as soon as the DA agrees it was self defense."

"I can testify to that," Jill said.

Phil smiled. "I think he'll take my word for it."

I pulled out my cell phone. "I'd better call my client, see if he wants me to talk to the media."

As I punched in Terry Tremont's number, Phil instructed the policeman to locate someone to come in and lock up the building. While I was explaining the situation to Terry, Vogel came back and said there were TV cameras outside.

"Did you talk to your newspaper friend?" Terry asked.

"We did, and he said he would work on the story. I need to call and tell him about this."

"My advice is you say nothing about working for me or for Protect Our Preds. The earlier story included the fact that Wechsel was an informant with some information for you. I'd suggest you say your investigation to find out what Wechsel had for you led to the NBA deal. The bomb that wrecked your car pointed to Franklin. When you confronted him, he confessed and threatened to kill you and Jill."

"That should work. Right now there're some TV people outside the building waiting for us to come out, but I don't want to upstage Wes Knight."

"Let the police handle it," Terry said. "Find a back door and dodge the cameras."

I switched off the phone and turned to Phil. "I guess you heard what I said. I promised the story to Wes Knight, who helped me out on Nick Zicarelli. Terry said to skip out the back door and let the police handle the TV guys. I like that advice."

Phil jammed his hands against his hips. "You want me to face that crowd of electronic leeches alone? They won't let go until they suck you dry."

"Tell them to talk to the department's spokesman," Jill said.

"I'd have to brief him."

"Call him now," I said. Then, grinning, I added, "You told me you don't like cops who spend a lot time in front of cameras. I don't want you despising yourself. Oh, one more thing. Terry Tremont asked that I not mention him hiring us on behalf of the Predator folks. He only wants me to say that our investigation into what Arnold planned to tell me led to the NBA deal, which is basically true."

Phil shrugged. "I won't mention Tremont's clients unless I'm asked. That's the best I can do."

"Fair enough," I said.

Phil called his PR man, who said he would brief the media at headquarters. Meanwhile, I got Wes at home and gave him the details of our confrontation with Franklin. I hated to admit that I had killed the man, but there was no way around it. The building manager arrived and turned off the lights inside so we could stay out of sight until it was safe to leave. Reluctantly, our detective friend went out to face the microphones. He gave a brief statement and sent them packing to the Criminal Justice Center.

35

WE BOUNDED OUT of bed early on Sunday morning to check the newspaper account of our Christmas Armageddon. It merited a bold headline at the top of page one. Wes and a team of reporters did a masterful job of tracking down multiple aspects of the case. Louie Aregis denied everything, but Wes had already talked with his former employee in Pensacola. He quoted portions of Gordon Franklin's confession regarding Nick Zicarelli's funding of Aregis' stake in the NBA consortium. He also mentioned that unnamed sources reported Coastal Capital Ventures was the target of a federal money laundering investigation.

At press time, Metro Police, assisted by the FBI, were raiding Nick Zicarelli's home in White House. They carried search warrants for gambling records. Grandpa was not available for comment. The most significant feature of the story for us came in a statement from Howard Hays, president of the Dollar Deal chain.

"Those of us who started the effort to bring a National Basketball Association team to Nashville have, from the start, been mindful of the necessity to protect the integrity of the sport. In consideration of this deplorable development, we have decided to withdraw from the proposed acquisition of an NBA franchise."

Fred Rickets of Physicians and Surgeons Software concurred in the statement. Louie Aregis had no comment.

While Jill and I sat at the kitchen table finishing our coffee with the last of the newspaper account, Phil Adamson called.

"I decided to apply a little pressure on the cell phone company last night after listening to Franklin on your recorder. They came through this morning with some interesting logs. There were several calls back and forth between Arnold Wechsel and Gordon Franklin. He had called Nicole Columbo the day he died. And calls with a cell phone listed to 'N. Zicarelli' ended a couple of days prior to Wechsel's death. Evidently old Nick wasn't as careful as we thought. Looks like you scored big on this one, buddy."

"Thanks, Phil," I said. "But you're the guy who provided the links. I should have given you everything we had a little sooner. Maybe a guy would still be around rather than in the morgue."

"He would've gotten what he had coming sooner or later. You did what you had to do. Put it aside and move on. I need you and Jill to come downtown and give your official statements."

I told Jill what we had to do, then shrugged. "Maybe the preacher will forgive us for missing one more Sunday." Instead of dressing for church, we donned our work clothes and headed for the Criminal Justice Center.

JILL SUGGESTED we follow up the closing of the case with a dinner for the people who had helped us the most, a practice we had followed after major successes. I was a bit skittish considering the way things had turned out Saturday night.

"It smacks of a celebration," I said. "I don't know if that would be proper with Gordon Franklin not yet cold in the ground."

She gave me a skeptical look. "I don't recall you having that problem after the Damon Saint affair last March."

She had me there. I guess things look different when it's your own foot in the shoe.

"Say when and I'll issue the invitations," I said.

With New Year's Eve coming up Friday, we decided on Thursday night. I invited Sam and Wilma Gannon, Terry and Roberta Tremont, Brad and Maruko Smotherman, and Phil and Liz Adamson. I thought about adding Wes Knight to the list, but after my previous experience with off-the-record comments to news people, I thought better of it. I did invite Mack Nelson, though I was sure he wouldn't come.

We took down the Christmas decorations and replaced them, thanks to a little help from the Predators' PR man, with a few pairs of ice skates, hockey sticks, and jerseys. Wilma came over early on Monday to help Jill get everything set up. Although hockey fans didn't tailgate, she decided to make it a strictly casual affair with barbeque pork and chicken, baked beans, potato salad, and all the rest. For desert, she had ice cream in the shape of hockey pucks. They were regulation size, one inch thick and three inches in diameter.

After everybody had arrived, we were seated at the table, about ready to eat, when the floodlight beep sounded. The doorbell rang by the time I got to the door. I opened it to find Mack Nelson standing there with his band leader, Deke Bragg, and the shifty-eyed security man, Rocky Topp.

"Sorry we're late," Mack said. "Hope there's still somethin' left to eat."

They set their guitar cases in the living room and joined us for dinner. Hockey talk dominated the evening. While we were eating dessert, Terry made a little speech, which is a nasty habit of lawyers, praising Jill and me for our dogged pursuit of the case.

I got up, bowed, and said, "I owe it all to my wife." And sat down.

Everyone applauded, except Jill.

She got up and said, "I have a lying husband." And sat down.

That brought a roar of laugher.

I had been dealing with a mix of emotions, and a pang of conscience prompted a sobering response. "In our euphoria over successfully closing the case," I said, "let's not forget the tragedy that led to the solution. Jill and I knew Arnold Wechsel as an ambitious young man looking forward to a bright future. He will be sorely missed by his family and friends."

That brought a long moment of silence. It was broken by Mack Nelson, who grabbed his cowboy hat off the back of the chair and plopped it onto his head. "If y'all will let us, we'd like to play you a little music."

With that, everyone adjourned to the living room and enjoyed an impromptu concert. It was late when the party broke up. Jill and I stood at the door and thanked each of them for their support in getting the case solved. Phil Adamson and his wife were the next to last to leave.

"I'm the one who should be giving the thanks," he said as he shook my hand. "You saved me a lot of work, buddy. But please don't wake me up in the middle of the night for awhile."

Jill grinned. "I'll keep him away from the phone after nine o'clock. I promise."

WHEN WE GOT TO church on Sunday, it was a new year and, I hoped, a new beginning. But after greeting a few people, I wasn't sure. I couldn't shake the feeling that I was being looked at differently than I had been before I shot and killed a man. Several offered condolences for what we'd been through.

John Jernigan remembered my interest in Gordon Franklin and said, "I had no idea it would be something like this."

"You gave me the key clue with that info about the Military Amateur Radio Service," I said. "That started all the pieces falling into place."

He gripped my arm. "I'm just thankful you got out of it alive."

Dr. Trent laid it all to rest with a comment during his sermon. Looking directly at me, he said, "Sometimes, in the face of crises, we are forced to take actions not of our choosing. On such occasions, it is important to make sure that what we do is always for the best of motives."

Looking around at Jill, I knew what had motivated me to make that fatal move. And I had no regrets.

9 780984 604401